Dylan laid a hand ... skin tingled.

His fingers traveled down her arm until he found her hand and clasped it within his own. "We've both been through the wringer today. And wherever Amy is, we won't find her at the Chesser homestead. If she was there, she'd have been found by now."

Bailey couldn't argue with his logic.

"Best thing we can do is chill out, get a good night's rest, then meet at dawn to start searching again."

He picked up the tin of salve and experimentally sniffed. "Makes me think of candy canes hanging on a Christmas tree."

"You should smell some of the other herbal concoctions." Bailey chuckled. "Especially the tinctures she wants you to drink."

Dylan scooped a dollop and then brushed her hair back from her left shoulder. "I see where he struck you."

He lightly applied more of the cooling salve and it helped numb the welt's heat, although it did set off a warmth in her core that had nothing to do with this morning's attack and everything to do with Dylan.

While I've tried to stay true to the Okefenokee Swamp's geography, certain liberties have been taken, such as the time it takes to travel from one location to another.

MURDER IN THE SHALLOWS

USA TODAY Bestselling Author

DEBBIE HERBERT

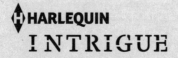

HARLEQUIN

INTRIGUE

Many thanks to all of you who have purchased this book! I hope
you enjoy reading this as much as I enjoyed writing it. It was such
a privilege to visit the Okefenokee Swamp while researching this
book and experiencing all of its wild beauty firsthand. I'd also like
to dedicate this book to my wonderful agent, Ann Leslie Tuttle of
Dystel, Goderich & Bourret LLC, for all of her encouragement on
this and every project we've worked on together over the years.

HARLEQUIN®

INTRIGUE®

Recycling programs
for this product may
not exist in your area.

ISBN-13: 978-1-335-13578-0

Murder in the Shallows

Copyright © 2020 by Debbie Herbert

Harlequin Enterprises ULC
22 Adelaide St. West, 40th Floor
Toronto, Ontario M5H 4E3, Canada
www.Harlequin.com

Printed in U.S.A.

USA TODAY bestselling author **Debbie Herbert** writes paranormal romance novels reflecting her belief that love, like magic, casts its own spell of enchantment. She's always been fascinated by magic, romance and gothic stories. Married and living in Alabama, she roots for the Crimson Tide football team. Her eldest son, like many of her characters, has autism. Her youngest son is in the US Army. A past Maggie Award finalist in both young adult and paranormal romance, she's a member of the Georgia Romance Writers of America.

Books by Debbie Herbert

Harlequin Intrigue

Appalachian Prey
Appalachian Abduction
Unmasking the Shadow Man
Murder in the Shallows

Harlequin Nocturne

Bayou Magic

Bayou Shadow Hunter
Bayou Shadow Protector
Bayou Wolf

Dark Seas

Siren's Secret
Siren's Treasure
Siren's Call

Visit the Author Profile page at Harlequin.com.

CAST OF CHARACTERS

Bailey Covington—She has the perfect job. As a park ranger stationed in the remote Okefenokee, she lives far from any neighbors and that's just the way she likes it. Years of neglect and abuse in the foster care system have left her unwilling to develop close relationships with others, especially men. She prefers the solitude and peace of the wild and mysterious swamp that's always provided a haven in storms of trouble. Her only goal in life is to live alone and enjoy nature while protecting the land and wildlife she loves.

Dylan Armstrong—He's a happy-go-lucky kind of guy who's proud of his family and their deep roots in the community. Like his father and grandfather before him, Dylan works in law enforcement and, despite his outward carefree attitude, he cares deeply about justice and ensuring the safety of the locals, known as "swampers," that he's been sworn to protect.

Lulu Atwell—A middle-aged Seminole woman who is a neighbor and friend to Bailey. She tells Bailey about the legends of the area and made her a talisman to protect her from evil.

Edgar Slacomb—Bailey's foster father who mistreated her in the past and is still a threat to her peace and safety.

Chapter One

Wild. Mysterious. Primordial.

Bailey throttled the ATV's accelerator, describing to herself the view she saw along Trail Ridge. She smiled in satisfaction as the wind whipped away the sweat clinging to her face and bare arms. Even though she hadn't discovered the Okefenokee Swamp until her teen years, she considered herself a true "swamper" in spirit, if not by birth. The primitive wildlife refuge had been a personal haven during her troubled adolescence, a place to soothe her battered mind and body. It still brought her peace.

An eagle soared above, its huge wings spread as it swooped down to the top of a nearby pond cypress. Quickly she gathered her binoculars for a closer look. An unfortunate squirrel dangled from the bird's marigold beak. But, hey, we all had to eat—including baby eaglets. As a park ranger, she'd often witnessed the relentless need to hunt or be hunted, to kill or be killed in the eternal quest for survival.

She brought the ATV to a stop and hastily noted the location and time in her log. Tracking eagles and gopher tortoises was a part of her duties in monitoring protected species. That done, she lifted her binoculars again in time to spot the adult eagle bringing the food to the giant nest that housed his mate and two eaglets.

Heat scorched her arms, and the humidity blanketed her skin. She swiped perspiration from her forehead and clutched the ATV keys, ready to move on.

Loud staccato warbling pierced the air, and several sandhill cranes soared upward, crashing through a clump of saw palmettos. Appropriately known as the "watchmen of the swamp," these birds let out a distress cry that alerted other creatures. More birds took flight, and even a couple of deer grazing along the blackwater shore went running for cover. Curious, she raised her binoculars and scanned the area from which they'd come but saw nothing unusual. Perhaps an alligator had lumbered near their nest. But normally, in that case, the cranes would hover above, squawking at and even swooping down on the gator to drive it away from their eggs or hatched babies.

Bailey hopped off the ATV and made her way down the embankment toward the wide, swampy patch of water that, several miles ahead, formed into a canal that led to the Suwannee River.

The sound of something dragging across the sand was followed by a loud swish of water. Perhaps she'd been right. It was a sunbathing gator returning to the water trail. Near the white sand shore, Bailey caught sight of the disturbance.

Not an alligator. It was a man. Dressed in camo, he navigated a long, slender johnboat, sluicing a paddle through the waters.

"Hey, there," she called out in a friendly greeting.

He didn't turn around, and she frowned. Why hadn't he answered? Was he illegally hunting gators or turtles?

"Hey," she called out again, determined to check his fishing license. "Hold up. Park management here."

His head turned slightly, allowing her to glimpse only a distant profile, but his olive-colored brimmed hat shaded the upper part of his face. Instead of turning around and obeying her command, he pulled the engine throttle and sped off.

Anger flushed her face. The man was definitely up to no good, but he had her at a disadvantage and knew it. She'd never catch up to him in the twisting, winding waters. Bailey pursed her lips, frustrated as he slipped out of reach.

By the time she fetched a boat, he'd have disappeared like a snake in high cotton. Her gaze swept the area, looking for a trotline or other signs of illegal activity, but there was only the drag mark of his boat in the sand and muddy footprints by the water's edge.

Her gaze traveled further, and she squinted at the railroad bridge, nearly overgrown by reeds and marsh grass. Had he gone for a hike on the Thirteen Bridges Trail? Usually, that place attracted a younger crowd drawn by the old ghost story—and a place to party. But she might as well take a look anyway and see if the mystery man had left any clues as to his identity.

It'd been months since she'd last walked the trail. She trod heavily on the near-rotten bridges—merely old crossties over wetland—and recalled the legend about a wailing woman searching for her lost baby. Supposedly she and her infant had been murdered out here not long after the Civil War.

Personally, Bailey thought it a bunch of nonsense, brought on by inebriated, highly suggestible kids—although she considered herself fairly open-minded about the supernatural. How could she not be? Her best friend, Lulu Atwell, was an older Seminole woman who told her tales of Native American lore that often defied rational explanation.

At the end of the trail, the tiny abandoned church still stood. She pushed open the door, surprised at its resistance. Given its age and condition, it should have been falling off its rusty hinges.

She squinted at the sudden darkness. Only two small grimy windows admitted filtered sunlight. Stale, moldy air twitched her nose. Her eyes adjusted, and she focused on two metal cots in the twenty-foot by thirty-foot room.

What the heck? This old place had always been empty, except for the occasional beer and liquor bottles strewn over the rough pine floor, relics from parties. But this?

Prickles washed down her spine as her mind immediately jumped to a story that had dominated the news for a couple of weeks. Two young women, sisters, had been reported missing. They were last seen kayaking away from the outfitter store in Folkston, Georgia—her town—located only seven miles southeast of an Okefenokee Park entrance.

This couldn't be related to those women—could it? No way.

Still, she couldn't shake off the weight of dread that crushed her lungs. Bailey squared her shoulders and marched to the beds. Thin, urine-stained mattresses lay atop the rusting cot frames, and she pulled up one of them.

A bundled strip of gray cotton was stuffed along one of the railings, looking like a mummified mouse.

Oh, no. As she looked at what appeared to be a gag cloth, bile rose in her throat, and her hand beelined for the leather sheath of her knife at her waist. But she wasn't thinking of the missing women. Instead, her mind leapfrogged to the past. As much as she'd suppressed those memories, they now flooded in.

And she was *there*. Sixteen years old and lying on the damp concrete basement floor, her face and body grinding into the cold concrete with its faint scent of mold. Above, the whistling snap of a belt before it descended. And as much as she tried to brace for it, she could never prepare for the burning sting. Or the screams muffled behind the dirty piece of cloth gagging her mouth.

No, no, no. That was long ago. I'm all grown up and safe. Even as she repeated the mantra to her trembling inner child, her body refused the comfort. Bailey ran out the door, leaned against the side of the church and vomited. That done, she breathed deeply—long, slow breaths—as she took in her surroundings. The eerie beauty and isolated environment of the swamp assuaged her anxiety as nothing else could. It was her sanctuary. Always had been, even during those dark days.

Resolutely she pushed away from the rotting

boards and squared her shoulders. Nothing could erase her past misery, but if someone had been hurt in this abandoned ruin, she'd do everything in her power to bring the abuser to justice.

Bailey pivoted, reentered the building, and went to work. A damn shame there was no cell service in this remote area, but her cell phone wasn't entirely useless. She dug it from her pocket and videoed the entire room from top to bottom. She noticed not another clue of foul play, but if this place was a crime scene, no doubt forensic experts would find microscopic details that she could not. And she was positive something bad had happened here. A heavy energy pervaded the church, seeping into her bones with the chill of certainty.

Briefly she debated collecting the gag cloth for safekeeping but decided against it. Best to let law enforcement gather it and keep it uncontaminated in their chain of evidence. It should be safe enough where it was. Unless… She recalled the man speeding away in the boat. Innocent outdoor enthusiast or illegal fisherman—or something worse? It was possible the man could return.

She shook her head and left the evidence as it was. Instead she walked around the building to check for anything else unusual. At the back of the church was a graveyard of over a dozen crumbling headstones with mostly unreadable etchings. A rusted metal fence sectioned off a patch of long-forgotten graves. Purple pickerel-weed and yellow-eyed grass choked the monuments to the dead.

Next to the cemetery was a maze of waist-high boxwoods that formed a labyrinth. Many believed that walking labyrinths was a gate to one's inner self, that its circular structure, combined with its spiral, meandering paths, led to a meditative peace and awareness. Had the mystery man traversed through here for his own nefarious purposes? Could there be another surprise in store?

In the interest of thoroughness, she'd take a look. Besides, she'd always been curious about the maze. She'd heard that no teenager, no matter how drunk, had ever dared to enter, as it was also—no surprise—believed to be haunted. General legend had it that to enter meant you'd be forever lost. No one returned alive.

Bailey entered the maze, boots scrunching against river pebbles that made up the path. Only a handful of weeds managed to push through the stones. The old English boxwoods that lined the maze were slightly overgrown but must have been a miniature variety not to have totally grown together over the years. Dutifully she walked the curves, searching left and right for foreign objects or anything out of place—a wrapper, a tissue, a sock. Soon, she'd reached the end of the labyrinth, where a large tea rose shrub bloomed at its center.

She inhaled the unexpected floral bouquet before her—but spiritual enlightenment? Nope. She felt none of that. Then again, searching for crime evidence probably emitted too many negative vibes, especially after the horrible memories that'd resurfaced only minutes ago. Turning to exit, she caught sight of silver glimmering from a nearby tupelo tree. What could this be?

Bailey pushed through one of the boxwoods and strode to the tree for a better look. The bit of silver flashed in the sun from high above, tantalizingly out of sight. Again, armed with the cell phone, she turned on the camera and zoomed in.

The lens of a small security camera blinked back at her.

Bailey gasped and took a step backward. "What the heck?" she muttered.

Nothing about this old chapel and graveyard was valuable. Besides, this was a wildlife refuge, not private property. No one had a right to set up surveillance equipment. Maybe it had been left to catch teenage trespassers? No, that didn't make sense. If park management had bothered to initiate security measures, she'd have been the one to install the camera and monitor its feed.

Which meant…she wasn't sure exactly what, but it couldn't be good. On its own, the discovery would have been perplexing, but when combined with the discovery of the cots, and the gag, it could only mean trouble.

And that man in the boat—was he connected to all this? Again, Bailey silently cursed that she hadn't had immediate access to her own boat.

What if you had? an inner voice taunted. *What might he have done to you?* She swallowed hard. Her mind leapfrogged to yet another dreadful realization. The man hadn't just seen her in person. She was now recorded on his camera. *Not like I'm defenseless,* she reminded herself, patting the knife at her waist. She was no longer a scared, trapped teenager at the mercy of her foster father.

The roar of a motor pierced the relentless cacophony of insects. She whipped around, trying to pinpoint the direction. The rumble came again, closer. Another ATV, she decided. Nobody was allowed to ride through here without specific authorization. So either this was another park employee or someone more ominous. Had the man in the boat circled around and landed? Was he now driving toward her?

One thing she knew for certain: she wasn't going to wait to find out. Bailey scrambled to the front of the church and sprinted toward her ATV parked near Trail Ridge, only twenty yards away. The other vehicle was almost upon her as she cranked the engine and hit the accelerator. If it turned out to be another employee, she'd look foolish, but for now, safety trumped pride.

Risking a quick glance in the mirror, she saw a man in dark sunglasses. The determined set of his jaw, along with the increased speed and direct aim of his ATV, told her that he meant to overtake her. The question was…why?

Unfortunately, the winner in this chase would come down to who drove the faster vehicle. Sadly, her decade-old, bottom-of-the-line ATV would be no match in this contest. The park had a limited budget, and speed was never a consideration in purchasing a serviceable ATV to roam the swamp.

He passed on the left and frowned, signaling her to stop.

Bailey tamped down her uneasiness as she regarded the interloper. He was dressed all in brown, some kind of uniform evidently, but not the park's. For the second time that day, she caught a glint of silver in the scorching afternoon sun. Only this time, she didn't need to zoom in with her cell phone to see it.

Pinned to the shirt on his right upper chest was a six-pointed star badge—the Charlton County Sheriff's Office. *Whew.* Bailey hit the brakes and jerked to a stop. How could they have known she was on her way to call them once she reached her cabin? Unless this area was already under suspicion and they were watching it. Which could explain the security camera. They might have placed it there in the hopes of nabbing a person of interest. Perhaps this officer observed the man exiting the chapel and then slinking off in his boat. Naturally he'd come to investigate.

The moment he turned off his ATV and faced her, Bailey quipped, "You're a day late and a dollar short."

His forehead creased, and he removed the dark sunglasses. Olive green eyes, the color of faded camo, regarded her in consternation. "Excuse me?"

"I said you're a little late. Your man's already slipped away by boat."

His frown only grew deeper. "Man? What man? I haven't a clue what you're talking about."

This time it was her turn to frown and regard him in confusion. Bailey cocked her head to the side. "Haven't you been watching the old church?"

He gazed over his shoulder at the abandoned structure and then faced her again. "Nooo," he said with a slow, deep drawl. "What makes you think that?"

"But…" She bit her lip, puzzled. In her seven years as a ranger, she'd encountered law enforcement officers only three times. Once, when a local child with autism had gone missing—thankfully, he'd been discovered hours later, unharmed and swimming in the alligator-and-snake-infested Suwannee River. The second time had been when a camper had suffered a heart attack, and his family had sent out an SOS flare in the dark of night. The third, of course, had been the recent massive descent of cops, firefighters and volunteers who had combed as much of the 438,000 acres as was humanly possible to search for the missing women.

"Why are you here then, Officer..." Her glance fell to the stitched letters under his badge, searching for a name. Horror closed her throat as she read it. *Dylan Armstrong.*

For the second time that day, the worst memories of her life resurfaced in an unexpected floodgate that, once opened, refused to recede. She hardly ever thought about that troubled time in her life, yet now, in the space of less than an hour, fate had punched her in the gut twice.

Coincidence?

Bailey believed in many things—that places like that old church contained a certain energy left from its history, that the Okefenokee held mysteries deep within its primitive fortress, that certain plants and animals often appeared at critical moments as messages from the universe.

But most of all she believed in signs—not co-incidence. And the fact that her past had twice been thrust in her face in rapid succession was a bad sign indeed.

"Ma'am, are you okay?" he asked, exiting his ATV and standing directly in front of her. He wasn't frowning now. Instead, his forehead was creased with concern. Those unusual olive-colored eyes—so like the elder Dylan Armstrong's she remembered—appeared kind and trustworthy, inviting her to accept his help.

But she wasn't going to be fooled. Not again. Not ever again.

He opened a bag tied to the back of his ATV and pulled out a water bottle, then thrust it into her hand. "Perhaps you're overheated? Dehydrated?" he suggested. "Happens all the time out here. Drink this, you'll feel better."

Anger replaced surprised horror and she shook her head. Did he take her for an incompetent idiot? For God's sake, she was an experienced ranger and knew to stay hydrated in the smothering heat. And even if she was thirsty, she'd never accept anything an Armstrong had to offer.

"I'm perfectly fine," she answered icily, effectively cutting off his overture. "What are you doing riding the land? Did you obtain a special permit?"

"Of course I did."

She'd just see about that. Bailey turned the ATV key and the motor roared to life. "Good day, Officer."

"Hey, wait a minute. What did you mean about the man speeding—"

His words were drowned out as she throttled the accelerator and the ATV wheels spun in the dirt, spraying clumps of soil onto his uniform pants. She watched him through the rearview mirror as he scowled at her, hands on his hips. But he made no move to follow, and the tightness in her chest eased as she drove around a bend and his tall form disappeared altogether.

She'd head straight to headquarters and report everything she'd seen at the church to her supervisors, as was her duty. In turn, it would be their responsibility to contact the sheriff with those findings. If Armstrong complained about her odd behavior today, she'd insist that she'd bypassed him in order to report everything directly to her own supervisors. The sheriff's office had their chain of command, and she had hers.

With any luck, she'd never have to set eyes on Officer Armstrong ever again.

Chapter Two

What the heck was that woman's problem?

Dylan brushed the dirt from his pants and climbed back on his ATV. He briefly considered overtaking her again—no doubt he easily could—but then what? Listen to more of her crazy talk? An encounter with a man had spooked her. His gaze drifted to the church. It stood abandoned as always. Another few years and the perpetual damp of the swamp, combined with the aggressive kudzu, would reduce the place to rubble.

His fingers twitched on the throttle. Annoyed as he was, he'd seen a moment of pure fear in her wide eyes. Come to think of it, he'd seen the woman around town a few times. Cool as ice, that one. He'd run into her at the grocery store once and had idly taken in her long, toned legs as she bagged apples in the produce aisle. Some sixth sense of being watched must have alerted her to his attention, and she raised her eyes, catching him gawking. Unfazed, he'd offered his customary breezy smile and waved. Instead of responding to his innocent flirtation with a smile—a reaction that, frankly, he was used to from women—she'd pulled her full lips into a tight line, abruptly turned her back on him and jerked her shopping cart in the opposite direction.

Jeff Aiken, his best friend since preschool, had hooted with laughter and nudged him with an elbow. "Don't think she was impressed with you, dude. You're losing your touch."

"Who is she?" he'd asked, checking out her shapely ass.

"Bailey something-or-other. Heard she works at the park and lives near it like a hermit. Not exactly friendly."

"That's a shame." He'd shaken his head, eyes still on the woman, lips curled in a rueful grin.

Jeff had grabbed a six-pack of beer and tossed it in his cart. "Stop acting like you're still in junior high, and let's get a move on."

The memory jogged him to action. Abruptly Dylan changed his mind and gave chase, the wind whipping his face as he accelerated. Bailey what's-her-name wasn't getting away so easily this time. If the ice queen was rattled, he wanted to know the reason.

In less than five minutes, he spotted her, riding

as fast as that run-down ATV could manage. He gunned the motor, and her head swung around for an instant before she faced forward again, never slowing. Dylan drew alongside her and motioned her to stop. Surprisingly, she obeyed. He exited his ATV and approached where she sat, her arms crossed and her lips pursed just as they were at the grocery store long ago.

"Appears we got off on the wrong foot, Bailey."

Surprise melted the stone-wall face, and she narrowed her eyes. "How do you know my name?"

He lifted his palms and shrugged. "Folkston's a small town. We bumped into each other once before."

"If you say so."

At her quirked brow, he realized she had no memory of the grocery store incident, which sent his ego into a nosedive. Still, he gave a determined smile, pushed the sunglasses to the top of his head, and held out a hand. "Dylan Armstrong, Charlton County Sheriff's Office."

She hesitated a moment, then reluctantly took his extended hand. He tried not to notice the effect of her smooth, warm palm in his grasp or imagine her sleek, tanned body hidden under the khaki uniform—it was hard enough not to stare at her exposed long legs in those shorts as she straddled her ATV.

"Bailey Covington," she said in exchange, withdrawing contact a beat too soon for politeness. At least she hadn't wiped her hand afterward.

"You didn't give me a chance to explain why I'm here," he said in his most professional voice, determined to keep his gaze from sweeping down to her legs. "I'm sure you're aware of the two women who've gone missing in the area. We're still searching as much ground as we can with limited manpower."

A shame that the chopper and boats they'd initially used had proved fruitless in the search. Too many places to hide in this wilderness.

"Of course I'm aware of the missing women."

"So, this mystery man of yours, do you think it's related?"

"Possibly. I'm on my way to make a report of what I found today, just in case."

He strove for patience. "Mind sharing?"

"I'm sure my supervisors will be more than happy to allow yours full access to the report. See you around, Officer Armstrong."

With that, she again started the ATV and took off in a cloud of dirt, leaving him staring after her.

Rude, yes. But instead of being irritated, he inexplicably grinned. Never one to back away from a challenge, Dylan flicked his sunglasses back down and returned to his ATV. "Go on and run. You haven't seen the last of me, Ranger."

WHEN DYLAN ARRIVED at the station, Jeff, his old friend and now a sheriff's deputy, glanced up from the paperwork on his desk and nodded at the sheriff's door. "Boss wants to see you ASAP."

Bailey's report must have already been filed and read. That was quick. Dylan knocked briefly on the closed door before striding inside.

Sheriff Franklin Chesser was frowning at his computer screen. "Weren't you patrolling today on Trail Ridge?" he asked with no preamble. "You didn't see any unusual activity?"

"Only an encounter with a closemouthed, annoying park ranger. I assume you're reading the report that she told me she would file with her boss?"

Chesser turned the monitor so that it faced him. "Take a look at this video she filmed."

Two bare metal cots were haphazardly strewed in the otherwise stark interior of the church. The lens zoomed in on a dirty strip of cloth lying on a rusted metal frame. The footage shook as Bailey Covington exited the church and scanned the area outside. The final shot was of a security camera perched in a nearby treetop. Then the monitor faded to black.

He and Chesser eyed one another uneasily.

"Think it has anything to do with the missing women?" he asked his boss.

"Can't help but make that leap." Chesser replayed the video, and they watched again in silence.

Chesser closed the video. "I have to be realistic, though. Could be squatters using the cots, and that camera might turn out to be a poacher's."

"Maybe," Dylan agreed.

A dubious silence hung in the room.

"Going to call in the state police again?" Dylan finally asked.

Chesser sighed and drummed his fingers along the scarred pine desk. Dylan understood his dilemma. When Mary Thornton and Amy Holley first went missing, it was determined they were last seen renting kayaks at an outfitting store at the Suwannee Canal entrance. State police had responded en masse. Dozens of them, along with local volunteers, had combed the river where the women had set off. Several boats and even a chopper had searched for six days.

All fruitless. They hadn't unearthed a single clue.

"Let's do some preliminary work first. I've already spoken with the park manager, Evan Johnson. You and the ranger who filmed this can work together collecting evidence and canvassing the area for more. Bring back that camera, and let's see what we've got."

"I don't need the ranger for any of that."

"It's called interagency cooperation, Dylan. Politics. Forging partnerships. Besides, she could prove helpful. Johnson claims she knows the swamp like the back of her hand."

"Not like I'd get lost out there," he muttered. "I've lived here all my life." It wasn't that he didn't want to see Bailey again—he did. But Dylan resented the implication that he *needed* her assistance.

"Johnson's the territorial type and wants his ranger to be involved in the investigation. Not a bad idea, either. If those women, or their bodies, are out there in the wilds, she'll know better than anybody how to track them. Take one of our dogs, too. See if you can pick up a scent."

"I could collect evidence a whole lot quicker without her," Dylan muttered again in protest.

"Go," Chesser said, using a voice that brooked no more argument. "Everyone else is busy catching up with other cases after spending so much time on the search. Bring back the evidence, and we'll take it from there."

"I'm on it." Dylan shoved to his feet.

"Thanks, kid," Chesser said gruffly. "You know I think of you as my right-hand man. Job will be yours one day soon. Your dad was one of the finest cops in the whole state of Georgia."

"No hurry." Dylan meant it, too. He was more than content to work as a deputy and learn all aspects of the job before running for sheriff. He'd already spent over three years on beat patrol and then five more years as captain of the K-9 unit before landing his current position. He wanted to win an election on his own merits, not on his late father's name and connections.

Dylan quickly collected a beagle, Ace, from the K-9 unit along with a plastic evidence bag filled with two swatches of the missing women's clothes. Ace settled into the cruiser with him, brown eyes dancing with excitement, muscles taut and quivering in anticipation.

"Going to earn your keep today, boy," he said, smiling at the beagle's happiness. Ace had always been his favorite dog to work with.

At the park entrance, he obtained special permission to borrow one of their jeeps and, beagle in tow, returned to the abandoned church. At least Ace was enjoying the outing. His black nose was lifted high in the air, taking in the scents, tail thumping loudly on the seat. Compared to being cooped up in a kennel, this was doggy nirvana.

The late-afternoon sun scorched Dylan's skin, and his dark brown uniform felt suffocating as he gathered the collection kit. Lucky for Bailey, her uniform was lighter colored, and she had the option of wearing shorts instead of pants. Speaking of the she-devil, Dylan spotted her slowly roaming the churchyard, mucking up footprints or whatever evidence might actually be at the scene. He suppressed a sigh and approached on foot, the beagle trotting at his side, eager to get to work.

Bailey watched them, no welcoming smile on her face for him or his dog. Evidently she wasn't thrilled to be working with them, either.

"We meet again," he said pleasantly.

"Might want to keep an eye on your dog," she replied in a flat greeting. "Hungry gators and venomous snakes, you know."

He kept his polite smile in place. "Nice to see you again, too."

"I'll show you where the camera's located."

Ace offered a friendly yip, but Bailey ignored him and abruptly turned, leading the way to the back of the church.

He trudged through the brackish plants, Ace close at his heel, sniffing away. Bailey came to a sudden standstill and pointed up at a tree. "There's the camera."

"Hold this for me a sec." He thrust the clothing sample bag and evidence kit in her hands.

"Why? What are you—"

"Going to take that thing in," he answered, snapping on a pair of plastic gloves and grabbing an empty baggie.

"You think that's wise?" she asked, frowning deeper and casting a wary eye on Ace.

"Did you think we'd just leave it here?" he asked,

eyeing the tree for a moment before he found a toehold and pushed up onto the first low limb.

"But if you take the camera, won't it spook the owner from returning?"

"Can't leave it and do nothing." Dylan climbed higher until he came eye level with the camera, which was fastened onto the end of a branch with zip ties. He dug a utility knife from his pocket and inched forward on the limb.

Ace barked and scratched at the tree, not happy at being left behind.

"You could do surveillance instead of removing the camera. See if he shows up again," Bailey suggested, shouting to make herself heard from several feet below.

"Kill me now," he muttered. She might not mind living and working outside in the boondocks, but as for himself, he couldn't imagine anything more miserable than camping in this snake-infested land, slapping at bloodsucking skeeters and biting flies all night in the suffocating humidity.

He popped open his knife blade and slashed through the tie, then carefully bagged the equipment before scrambling back down the tree. Bailey's hands were on her hips, her look reproachful.

"Hey, if you want to hang around here day

and night to see if someone shows up, then more power to you," he said.

"Maybe I will."

She lifted the chin of her heart-shaped face, a stubborn gesture he secretly found more amusing than annoying.

"Don't get any wild ideas," he warned. "It's not safe for you to attempt something dangerous out here all by yourself."

"And to think I've managed this job on my own just fine for the past seven years."

"Have you ever been out in the wilds with a possible kidnapper before?"

"Well…no. Not that I'm aware of, anyway. But who knows what lurks out there?"

Apparently the woman hated to admit a possible vulnerability, but Dylan had to allow that he was the same. "I'm not questioning your courage," he said gently. "Not many people—man or woman—are cut out to work in a swamp full of reptiles."

Something fierce flashed in her eyes before she shuttered an emotion brewing below the surface. "My guess is that the reptiles are far safer than some humans." With that cryptic remark, she nodded at Ace. "Want to check out the church before your dog roams further out?"

"Sounds like a plan."

He followed her to the front of the building,

doing his best to keep his eyes from drifting down and staring at her butt, and keep his brain focused on the job at hand. As Jeff had once said, he wasn't in junior high anymore. Not like he hadn't seen plenty of action over the years, either. Maybe it was Bailey's total lack of interest in him that roused a primitive need to make her respond to him.

Inside the church, he breathed a sigh of relief at the slight drop in temperature. Ace trotted past them both to get to the cots. Bailey hastily swept to the side to avoid the brush of fur against her legs.

Sudden understanding flashed. "Are you afraid of dogs?" he asked.

Her reply was much too swift and charged with vehemence. "'Course not."

She was lying.

"Ace, come," he demanded, snapping his fingers and pointing to the door.

The little beagle swiftly complied, even if his chocolate eyes protested the order. Ace planted himself in the doorway, his body taut, eagerly awaiting the signal to search. Dylan faced Bailey in time to catch the slight whoosh of breath escaping her throat, signaling relief.

Keep Ace from drawing too near Bailey again, he mentally noted. Ace would never harm her, but even if he told her so, it wouldn't take away her fear. Whatever encounter she'd had with a dog in the past, it must have been bad to be leery of a beagle—they were like the teddy bears of dog breeds.

Bailey cocked her head at the cots. "What do you think? Suspicious or not?"

"The sheriff suggested it might be squatters or hunters using this place. Catch many trespassers out here?"

"It happens. But it's not hunting season, and I've never come across something as permanent as cots. It's always blankets or sleeping bags."

She stepped to one of the cots and leaned over, pointing at the strip of cloth on the metal frame. "And then there's this."

Dylan gathered the cloth, placed it in a separate baggie and took close-up photos of everything.

"My fingerprints are on the mattresses," Bailey admitted. "I flipped them over looking for clues."

"I'll make a note of it and get your fingerprints, so we can rule you out in a search." He dusted black powder along the metal frames and mattresses, then stood and scanned the room. There were traces of dusty footprints inside, but they were blurred and of all sizes. Nothing distinctive. This place must still be a hangout for bored teenagers.

"Maybe the cots are for—" he hesitated a beat and plunged on "—you know, overly hormonal teens using this place to party."

Skepticism etched Bailey's face. "Kids today don't use it near as much as they did back in my day. But I understand that particular motive can't be ruled out."

Had she ever used this location for such a purpose? he wondered. But he tamped down his curiosity with determination.

"Now what do we do?" she asked.

"Time to let Ace do his thing."

Dylan swore the beagle grinned in happy anticipation. He withdrew the bag containing the cloth swatches. Bending on one knee, he held the swatches out, and Ace's black nose twitched as he sniffed experimentally.

"Seek," he commanded.

Ace made a beeline to the cots and whimpered as he placed his paws on the mattresses and barked.

"Bingo," Dylan whispered. This was the first big break in the case—and an ominous one at that. But after two weeks, no one expected the women to show up unscathed.

"Those women were here, then," Bailey softly stated, eyes focused on Ace.

"Appears so. I'll load the mattresses onto the jeep, and at the station, we'll cut them open to see if there's anything inside. We'll also check for blood and other DNA markers."

"I want to be there when you do."

He shrugged. "Suppose that's fine. Your boss made it clear he wants you involved in the investigation. But lab samples will be sent to Atlanta, and our forensics sample work is usually undramatic."

"I didn't know that. Just inform me if there's any major finding, then."

"Of course. I'm going to have Ace sniff around outside and see what we can find."

This time, Dylan led the way. The beagle ran past him and, nose to the ground, drew them to the side of the building and then behind. Ace methodically made his way to the labyrinth.

"I did a quick walk-through earlier," Bailey offered. "Nothing jumped out at me, but there could be something small I missed."

Bees happily hummed around the gallberry plants and swamp gum trees, oblivious to the violence that had potentially been perpetrated in the maze. But he was getting ahead of himself. Perhaps the women had merely made a pit stop along the riverbank when they spotted the church and then had simply explored the area.

At the dead end, Ace hurried to the blooming tea rose bush and frantically began digging. White sand sprayed into the air.

A buried body or two, perhaps?

Unguarded, Bailey glanced at him, her brows raised and her blue eyes filled with dread.

"Why don't you wait for me in the church?" he suggested.

Wordlessly, she shook her head and switched her gaze back to Ace's frantic pawing. Slivers of gold glinted in the waning sun. Dylan knelt and picked up a thin chain with his gloved hands, recollecting a detail from the case. Both of the missing kayakers had been wearing gold necklaces. One had a cross on it, and the other woman's had a claddagh. He'd bet anything there was a murderer on the loose and in possession of both those charms.

"A trophy," he breathed.

Bailey was beside him, her shoulders brushing against his. The contact warmed the cold chill that had prickled down his spine.

"I thought killers kept trophies to relive their crimes," she said.

"They do. Not sure why a chain was left behind and buried. If this is a trophy, and we don't know that it is, the suspect will have some warped reason in his sick head. Maybe to mark the spot where he killed one or both of them."

"As good a reason as any, I suppose." He felt her tremble beside him. "Though I'm still going to hold out hope both women are alive."

He held no such optimism. Not that he needed it to sustain him in a serious crime investigation. Instead, it was the need for justice that drove him.

Work completed, Ace lay down and awaited the praise due him.

"Good boy." Dylan patted him and then rolled the necklace in the palm of his gloved hand before sealing it in an evidence bag. The sun beat down on his back, and the honeybees droned as they collected nectar. The scent of roses perfumed this unholy spot where two women might have met their death. He and Bailey grew quiet, a shared moment of respectful silence.

Violent death had possibly marked this spot. Now to test that theory and stop a killer before he struck again.

Chapter Three

"Sounds like a tough day. A creepy day."

As usual, Miss Lulu succinctly summed up everything in her tidy, no-nonsense way. Bailey rocked on the older woman's front porch glider, bare feet dangling, and sipped from a mason jar of sweet tea. In the deepening twilight, fireflies danced and glowed like drunken pixies. For the first time in hours, she felt relaxed.

"It wasn't the most fun I've ever had at work," she allowed.

"Could be dangerous," Lulu warned. "You living alone in the middle of nowhere."

Bailey snorted. "You've been doing the same most of your life. Besides, we have each other for neighbors."

Their cabins were nearly a quarter mile apart, and Bailey was glad to have her as a neighbor. They were kindred spirits, even if over three decades apart in age.

Lulu nodded, smoothing back her black hair

shot through with silver. "And we have our shot-guns. In case of trouble."

Bailey dearly hoped she'd never have need to use the weapon. Until a couple of weeks ago, she'd only imagined raising it in case of an encounter with an aggressive black bear.

Much as she'd enjoyed the evening and the supper of duck fried rice and collards, it was time to shove off. Lulu always retired early and rose with the sun.

"I'll get the dishes," Bailey offered. As Lulu started to stand from the rocker, Bailey gestured for her to stay. "I've got it. Least I can do after all your cooking."

Ignoring Lulu's grumbling, Bailey reentered the cabin. She filled the chipped enamel sink with hot water and a squirt of dishwashing liquid. Truth be told, she enjoyed washing dishes. As her hands soaked in the warm water and fragrant pink dishwashing liquid, she gazed out the window. It was like a prayer, a meditation, as she cleaned and rinsed each plate before placing it, glistening, in the drying rack. But the piercing headlight beams of an approaching truck dispelled her peace. This wasn't exactly a hospitable stretch of road she shared with Lulu. Unpaved and wracked with deep mudholes, it led nowhere.

Faint consternation gave way to deep misgiving when the truck stopped abruptly halfway between her and Lulu's cabins.

"Expectin' company?" Lulu asked, entering the kitchen to stand by her side.

"Not hardly. You?"

They both watched and waited, but no one emerged from the vehicle.

"Nope. I don't like this," Lulu muttered. "Not after what you found in the church today."

"Where are your binoculars? I can't make out who it is."

"Binoculars, heck. I'm gettin' my shotgun."

"No need for all that," she chided, though she'd be lying if the thought of a loaded weapon didn't offer some comfort. "Let's see what we're dealing with."

Lulu reluctantly thrust the binoculars into her hands.

Bailey raised them. At the familiar shock of sandy hair, she groaned.

"Who is it?"

"One of Charlton County's finest. Name's Dylan Armstrong."

"What's he doing parked here?"

"That's what I aim to find out."

Lulu's dark eyes narrowed. "You sure it's safe?"

Another reason she felt close to this woman. Their mutual mistrust of lawmen. Lulu had never enlightened Bailey as to the exact reason for her mistrust, but she'd assumed Lulu had suffered from the same callous treatment she'd once received while seeking help from the law. Treatment she'd experienced thanks to Deputy Sheriff Dylan Armstrong *Senior*.

There it was. A third time in one day that she'd been forced to recall a past she'd rather forget.

"Everything's fine," Bailey assured her. "I'll send him on home."

"Take this with you." Lulu nodded at a covered plastic bowl filled with leftovers.

"You don't have to—"

"Take it."

"Still got enough for Holt if he drops by later?"

"Maybe. He was due to finish his latest tour yesterday. Haven't seen hide nor hair of him today though."

Holt Rucker, Lulu's special friend, worked as an expedition guide through the swamp and other wilderness areas. His schedule was erratic, but it seemed to suit his needs and unencumbered lifestyle. "Surprised he isn't already over," she said.

Lulu raised a brow but didn't comment. Bailey couldn't figure out the exact nature of their relationship. Holt often slept over, but Lulu refused to categorize him as a boyfriend and never complained about their casual arrangement. Evidently, the older generation had their own version of "friends with benefits."

"I made plenty of food."

Bailey knew when she was beaten. "Yes, ma'am. Guess I'll head on back and tell my stalker to hit the road."

Outside, the scent of gardenias and honeysuckle wafted through the air, soothing her jitters at the coming confrontation. She'd barely made it to the dirt road when his engine turned over and the headlights cut through the darkening sky. What was he doing out here? She hadn't asked for protection. Unless there was some break in the case already?

The truck skidded to a stop by her side, and the passenger door flung open.

"Hop in, Bailey. I'll give you a lift."

"Why are you here?" she asked bluntly. "Any news on the missing women?"

"I wish."

She stood unmoving. "Then why?"

He ran a hand through his hair. "Just keeping an eye out for you. Saw you head over here so I parked halfway, trying to keep an eye on both cabins. Don't get all huffy."

"There's no need." She didn't want to be beholden to any man, especially this one.

"Come on, Bailey. You know better. You were seen today."

"From afar. My hair was pulled back in a ponytail, and my hat kept my face shaded."

"Still, there can't be that many female forest rangers in the park. Correct?"

"Just me," she begrudgingly admitted.

"Shouldn't be too hard to get your name from the park website, and then…" He let his voice trail, allowing her to follow the silence to its logical conclusion.

She had to admit that Dylan was right. With the internet, nothing seemed safe or private these days.

"I have a shotgun. I'm good."

"Okay. Just humor me, then. Get in the truck, and I'll save you a few steps."

Sighing, Bailey climbed in. If she didn't, she'd be arguing with him all night. At least that yipping dog wasn't on board. True, the beagle had sported a friendly, eager face, nothing like her foster father's trained attack Dobermans, but she respected that the animal still had a mouth full of sharp teeth. Once bitten, forever shy.

Dylan whipped the truck around, and she balanced the plastic dish in her lap as they rumbled toward her cabin, which was almost as rustic as Lulu's—with the exception that Bailey's had an air-conditioning unit. After a long day of patrolling the wildlife refuge, the last thing she wanted was to return to a hot, stuffy cabin in the evening.

He parked in front of her house and stared into the gathering darkness.

"Now what?" she asked.

"You invite me in?"

She let out a laugh. "Are you seriously inviting yourself to spend the night?"

"Not the way it sounds." Even in the dark, she detected a flush on his neck and face.

"Go home, Dylan. We might be working together, but I don't know you well enough for sleepovers, and your truck's going to get mighty uncomfortable."

"Wouldn't be my first stakeout. I'll survive."

Stubborn, stubborn man. She opened the door and slid out. Guilt pricked her for an instant, but she hardened her heart. If he wanted to act like a fool, that was on him. "Have you even eaten supper?"

Immediately she wanted to kick herself for asking. This wasn't her problem.

He picked up a bag of trail mix from the dashboard and rattled its contents. "A complete meal of protein, carbs and fats."

Impulsively, she thrust the plastic container at him. "Here's real food. If you don't have any plastic utensils in your truck, I can bring you out some."

"I'm all set." Dylan flipped open the glove box, revealing a stash of napkins, salt and pepper packets, a bottle of hot sauce and plastic forks. "Never know when these might come in handy."

Her conscience clear, Bailey shut the door. "Still say you should head on home."

She felt his eyes on her as she walked across the yard and opened the cabin door.

"Might want to start locking up your place," Dylan called out.

Bailey didn't bother responding. He was right, but she'd managed to figure that out on her own without his advice.

Was she really at risk? The unknown man had viewed her from a distance, after all. He'd seen her general body shape and long hair pulled into a ponytail. In the bedroom, Bailey let down her hair in front of the dresser, letting the brown locks flutter a good six inches past her shoulders. She was past due for a haircut, anyway. Bailey retrieved a pair of scissors and commenced cutting.

Five minutes later, she critically surveyed her handiwork. It would do. The bobbed length lay halfway between her chin and ears. A practical summer cut that would be cooler and also fit her wash-and-let-it-be style.

Like most evenings, Bailey plopped into bed and read, although tonight getting into the book proved difficult. Every so often, she swept aside the curtain and spotted Dylan still parked outside in the truck. At last, she turned out the light, determined to fall asleep. The morning work would start at dawn.

Familiar night noises of cicadas, frogs and owls lulled her unease. She touched the leather cord around her neck and ran her fingers over the charms Lulu had strung on it for blessing and protection—a crow feather for strength, power and wisdom, two turquoise beads representing friendship and an obsidian arrowhead for a hunter's alertness. Four items total, four being a powerful number symbolizing the four moon phases. As she sank into the gray oblivion of sleep, she hoped they'd keep her safe.

EXCITED BARKING.

The pungent scent of wet fur, an ominous growl and then nearby panting. Hot kibble-breath.

The dogs were almost upon her.

Bailey sprang to wakefulness, cotton bedsheets clutched in her hands. Blood pulsed in her ears as she searched the darkness for her location. She was home. Safe in her own room. Quickly she rose and went to the kitchen for a glass of water. As the tap filled her cup, she stared out the window over the sink. Moonglow tinged the trees and grass with a silver hue. With a start, she remembered Dylan and padded over to the den to look out the front window.

His truck was in the same spot, but she couldn't see him. Perhaps he'd lain down in the seat to sleep? Some protector. Come morning, she'd be sure to give him a hard time. Her hand found the smooth barrel of the shotgun she kept lodged near the front door. Its hard, cool surface reassured her that she could take care of herself if need be.

Instead of returning to bed, Bailey threw on a T-shirt and shorts and headed to Dylan's truck, determined to send him home. If he drove off now, he could still catch a few hours' sleep in a comfortable bed before they began another search. She rapped sharply on the driver's side window. "Dylan?" she called, not wanting to scare him—not too bad, anyway.

No answer. Man slept like the dead. What kind of cop did that on a protection detail? She peered into the back seat.

Empty.

Chills skittered down the back of her neck and spine. She slowly turned to face the cabin. A man was crouched near the swamp hibiscus by the east wall. Dylan? Impossible to make out from the inky shadows. An urge to angrily confront him warred with the fear that this might be someone else entirely. Although, did it matter who lurked there? What did she really know about this Dylan Armstrong? Precious little. Except for the fact that his father had been a nogood, heartless liar who'd turned his back on a terrified teenager who'd sought his help.

She cursed herself for not taking her shotgun. A weapon was no good if she forgot to carry it in the middle of night. Especially after she'd been warned she might be in danger.

The figure straightened and approached. He stepped away from the shrubs and into the wide expanse of the lawn, and the moonlight glinted on his sandy hair.

"What are you doing outside, Bailey?"

As if he had the right to question her movements. Resentment coupled with a healthy dose of cynicism kept her on guard. "What are *you* doing creeping around my cabin?" she countered.

He was close enough now that she saw the flicker of annoyance in his eyes. Well, he was no more irritated than she. Dylan had no business—

"Someone was out here," he said, cutting into her indignant thoughts. "I saw movement and heard noise in the shrubs. Which, by the way, are way too tall and need trimming. A giant could hide in that jungle."

She ignored his bossy commentary and cut to the chase. "What noise?"

"A rustling not caused by the wind. I climbed out of my truck, and whoever it was took off for the woods out back. You didn't hear me yell for him to halt?"

No, there'd only been the nightmare.

"So, he got away," she breathed, uselessly fixing her gaze on the dark tree line.

"At least I noticed him before he torched your cabin."

Her heart skipped and squeezed at that bit of news. "How do you know his intention?"

Instead of answering, Dylan motioned for her and walked back toward the cabin. Through the damp grass, she followed, arms hugged about her waist. Within ten yards of the shrubs, she halted abruptly. A gasoline odor permeated the night air, overpowering the sweet smell of honeysuckle and gardenia. Under one of the shrubs was a discarded gas container.

She rubbed her arms against the wave of cold that swept her from head to toe. If Dylan hadn't been here...

Unless *he'd* been the one who doused her cabin with gasoline.

She tried to think rationally, warring between what was either paranoia or a healthy suspicion. But why would Dylan have done such a thing? Yeah, she had no use for his father, but it didn't mean that the son was a killer trying to deflect suspicion from his murderous secrets by playing a hero.

"I guess thanks are in order," she said reluctantly.

A rueful smile played on his lips. "Must have killed you to say that."

Chapter Four

Bailey sipped coffee as she and Dylan peered down at the huge map spread out on the conference table at park headquarters. The park land was vast. Over seventy islands dotted the map, along with two major rivers and a stream of waterways twisting throughout the Okefenokee.

"What, exactly, are you looking for?" Dylan asked. His tone was less than pleasant. He slouched in a chair, legs sprawled before him. A sexy stubble—Bailey couldn't help the errant thought—graced his jaw, which he wearily rubbed.

She probably looked every bit as discombobulated as Dylan, but she'd never admit to anyone just how shaken last night's events had left her. Either she was a random victim or a possible killer knew her identity. Regardless, after the cabin was nearly torched, they'd left immediately and had come to the park headquarters.

"Not a morning person?" she asked Dylan with fake cheer.

"It's not morning yet." He yawned, glancing out the bank of dark windows on the east wall.

"Sure it is. I see a few sun rays on the horizon." Bailey took a perverse pleasure in antagonizing him. "Why don't you go home, shower and change clothes?"

"I've got clean clothes in my truck. Is there a place to shower in this building?"

"Yep. I'll show you where it is."

"It can wait until a few employees show up."

Did he plan to stick to her like glue until the suspected kidnapper was found? Heaven help her. "Suit yourself," she said with a shrug, turning her attention back to the map. "To answer your earlier question, I'm looking for a hiding place."

Were the missing women still alive—or at least one of them? After all, there was a gold chain unaccounted for, which bugged Bailey. Why did the kidnapper only bury one of the necklaces in the labyrinth?

Where else could he have taken a victim? She stared at the map and shook her head in despair. So many places to hide. The swamp offered a wealth of opportunity for someone knowledgeable of its twisting secrets.

Not to mention the twelve thousand alligators that called this area home, any one of which could easily drag a human body to the bottom of the swamp and feast, leaving only the bones scattered beneath the blackwater's calm surface.

She couldn't dwell on that depressing reality.

"What's the sheriff's office's game plan for today?" she asked.

"They'll send out more officers and a few cadaver dogs to better comb the Thirteen Bridges area. They've already sent your findings to the forensics lab in Atlanta. Boss put in a request that they expedite the tests. We'll see."

"Think there's anything stuffed in those mattresses?"

"No. They already checked." He held up a hand, warding her off. "I know you said you wanted to be there, but we'd had a long day and—"

"It's fine."

Dylan tapped his knuckles against the map. "Got any ideas on where to go from here?"

She slowly sat down across from him, clutching the warm coffee mug between her palms. "Depends. Anything you can share about the investigation that hasn't been reported to the media?"

"Unfortunately, no. As reported, when the women went missing, we didn't rule out foul play. Their overturned kayaks were found almost nine miles from the outfitter store, in a side waterway off the Suwannee River." Dylan squinted at the map and then pointed a finger. "Right there."

Bailey dutifully marked the spot with a black Sharpie.

"The women were experienced kayakers," Dylan continued. "Friends and family swore they always carried compasses and used them for navigation."

"And now we're close to proving there was foul play."

"That being the case, we always suspected the kidnapper was someone local and familiar with the area."

"Of course. So, this man possibly likes to keep women hostage in sheltered, remote areas. Apparently gagged and maybe bound in some way." She didn't even want to think what he did with them as they lay helpless.

"That appears to be what we're now dealing with." Dylan poured more coffee. "But why now? There've been no other violent crimes connected to the park."

"Could be this guy's first offense," she suggested.

"Maybe," he said, though his doubtful scowl indicated that he didn't agree with this theory.

"If so, then it sounds like we're describing a younger man. Someone who's never before acted on his violent urges." She paused. "Or someone who's cleverly covered up his past crimes until now. Have you had reports of other missing persons in this area?"

Dylan hesitated. "People disappear from time to time. Runaway teenagers, spouses who up and leave their significant other with no trace. Most of these cases are quickly resolved. But the wildlife refuge cuts through miles of the Georgia-Florida border, which encompasses a large number of people. It's entirely possible there are open missing person cases. What are you suggesting?"

"That Mary Thornton and Amy Holley might not be the first victims."

The theory lay bare before them—tantalizing and horrific.

"Can't help wondering if more trophies lie buried, scattered about like his personal treasures." Her own words made her shiver.

From the front door came the harsh sound of metal scraping metal—a key turning in the lock.

Dylan leaped to his feet, all semblance of exhaustion erased. His hand went to his sidearm as he rushed to the door.

"If they're using a key, they must work here," she said, tamping down a burst of adrenaline, even as her hand reached for the knife at her belt.

"Or it's somebody picking a lock."

Dylan flattened himself against the wall by

the door and motioned for her to do the same. The gun's safety lock clicked off, and he held it in his right hand, finger on the trigger.

Another jiggle of the key, and the door squeaked open. A tall, rangy man dressed in khaki stepped inside. Her boss. Bailey let out a heavy breath and strode to the door. "Evan! You're here early."

Thick brows rose on his rugged, tanned face. His skin showed the signs of a lifetime spent outdoors, but even so, it didn't detract from his appeal. Close-cropped white-silver hair emphasized cornflower blue eyes. He flashed a grin, perfect white teeth gleaming against olive skin.

The grin died the moment he spotted Dylan holstering his weapon. "You must be the deputy that Chesser assigned to work with Bailey."

"Correct." Dylan's face was guarded, his eyes suspicious. "You always arrive so early to work?"

If Evan noticed the lack of warmth from the cop, he showed no signs of offense. "Not every day we're called in on a criminal case. How's the investigation going?"

Bailey quickly filled him in.

"Where do we go from here?" Evan asked. "Wait for forensic confirmation that the necklace belonged to one of the women?"

"We've put in a rush request to have the prints

and DNA tested, but it could take days. Weeks, even. The office is chronically short staffed."

"Sounds like there's nothing more to be done." Evan nodded at Bailey. "Ready to report back to your regular duties?"

"No." It wasn't like she wanted to spend more time with Dylan and his yippy beagle, but if there was the slightest possibility that one of the women was alive, she had to continue to search.

Both men regarded her with raised brows.

"I'd like a few more days to search."

"Search for what?" Evan asked.

Dylan's eyes flashed with understanding, and he gave a slight nod. "There was only one necklace found. So where's the other?"

"Exactly," said Bailey. "Couldn't hurt to check out a few more places. The kidnapper's shown he takes advantage of old structures to hide his victims." *Until he kills them.* She pushed the disquieting thought away. "He's obviously familiar with the area, so he'd know where there are plenty of old cabins and sheds." She paused a moment when the thought hit her. "Like on Billy's Island."

"Wouldn't that be too obvious? Too risky?" Evan asked, frowning. "The place is popular with tourists."

"Only the western end of the island," she objected. "On the opposite side are several rusted metal sheds and a couple pine buildings left abandoned from the old timber company."

Evan's lips pressed tightly together. "Needle in a haystack."

Her spirits sank. He wasn't going to let her continue assisting the law enforcement officers. How could she return to the same old duties when her talents and knowledge of the area could help solve this case?

"The sheriff's office is game," Dylan said. "If your agency is no longer interested in participating in a joint search-and-rescue venture, I'm sure Sheriff Chesser will understand. Although, it'd be a shame not to have Bailey's assistance. I wasn't even aware of those abandoned structures on Billy's Island."

Very slick. Dylan had appealed to her boss's pride. Grateful as she was for his tactic, it served as another reminder to be wary of the guy. His open, boyish face and manner didn't mean there weren't a few tricks up his sleeve.

Evan held up a hand. "Never let it be said we didn't provide y'all our full cooperation in this matter. Bailey, you're free to work with them over the next week. After that, check in with me, and we'll decide where to go from there."

"No time like now." She cocked her head at Dylan, eager to be on their way before Evan changed his mind. "There're sandwiches in the break room fridge. Let's pack a lunch."

By THE TIME they picked up Ace and settled into the small motorboat, sunrise was in full bloom, its coral rays brightening a path down the winding water trails. The coffee-colored water, infused with tannin, was dark but clear. The stream was only three feet deep, yet the current was strong and pulsing beneath the boat's floorboard.

Bailey sat at the helm, navigating the narrow lane bordered by lily pads—all while keeping a wary eye on Ace. Every minute, the stubborn dog edged a tad closer, creeping forward on his belly, brown eyes earnest with longing.

"He's very well behaved," Dylan offered.

"So you say," she grumbled, angling her legs away from the pup. "Keep him by your side."

Dylan patted his leg, and Ace scooted back by his feet. "I'm curious. Are there many places in the swamp that have old abandoned buildings?"

"Several. There's the old Chesser homestead and Floyd's Island. A few other locations off the beaten path as well. We used to have more but the forest fire in 2011 wiped them out."

"Everything in the swamp is off the beaten path. Any special reason we're going to Billy's Island first?"

She glanced at him from the corner of her eye,

debating whether to reveal her other reason. He'd no doubt find her amateur theory amusing. After all, she was a forest ranger, not a detective.

"Go on," he urged. "I'm listening."

Bailey touched the obsidian arrowhead that lay against her breastbone, then skimmed the crow feather and turquoise beads. So what if he laughed at her idea? Her self-worth wasn't based on anyone else's opinion—especially not one named Armstrong.

"Maybe one of the reasons he used the church is because there's such a strong legend around it. Lots of folks are afraid of the place."

"Not the teenagers who use it to party," he pointed out.

"They don't use it much anymore. Not like when I was growing up around here. The place is mostly avoided. And then there's the labyrinth, where he buried at least one token." She hesitated.

"Go on," he prodded.

"Maybe he has a bizarre sense of the holy, or a need to defile sacred places."

Dylan rubbed his chin and then gave a quick nod. "Are you thinking of the Native American mound at Billy's Island?"

Just then, the oak platform dock emerged from around the bend, and she steered toward it. "Yes.

Plus, the island also has its share of supernatural tales and resident ghosts."

"Chief Billy from the Seminole tribe. I know that one." Dylan chuckled. "Supposedly he was murdered here and comes back to haunt unsuspecting campers."

Their boat bumped against the dock, and she expertly tied a rope around a metal cleat to secure it. "Don't forget about Bigfoot, the Skunk Ape and the South Georgia Pig Man," she added.

"Not to mention UFO sightings and alien abductions. Got it."

A reluctant grin tugged her lips. He was surprisingly easy to get along with, so she'd have to keep her guard up.

She climbed out of the boat with the metal detector and trowel, while Dylan exited carrying Ace and an evidence kit in his arms. He had the dog once again sniff a bag containing clothing samples from the missing women, and her passing amusement vanished.

They stepped onto land, and her boots sank an inch in the damp, unstable peat deposits. Native Americans called the swamp "land of the trembling earth" for just this reason. It made for inconvenient footing, but still, she loved the smell of the wet bog, and this brief stretch of morning before the smothering heat and humidity descended like heavy blankets.

"Should we go to the Native American mound first?" Dylan suggested.

"That works. We can check that and the cabins before hiking over to the old industrial area."

Ace darted ahead of them, eager for the day's hunt. And it would be grueling work. The island was four miles long and one and a half miles wide.

"I can't help thinking about that lost man," she blurted.

Dylan faced her, grimacing. He apparently knew exactly what she was talking about. "Strange things happen out here, no denying that."

Swampers still remembered the lost man. In 1996, he was lost for forty-one days in the swamp, despite a massive search that included helicopters equipped to detect infrared body heat. Finally, he emerged on Billy's Island, dehydrated, confused and exhausted. Theories ran rampant. A few of the crazier ones suggested an alien abduction that resulted in a memory wipe.

Ace quickened his pace as they approached the deserted village. Nearly five hundred people once lived and worked there in a doomed timber operation at the turn of the last century. The swamp eventually defeated all efforts at industrialization, and Bailey couldn't be sad about that. Too many magnificent cypress trees had been hauled away.

Although most of the old homes had gone up

in flames, rusty bathtubs remained as well as other relics—a silent testament to the hardy folks who'd tried to tame the wild land. Ace eagerly sniffed each of the tubs, his twitching nose low to the ground. Occasionally his head rose, and he lifted his nose high, discerning some new bewitching scent to be investigated.

Bailey turned on the metal detector and absently arced it over the ground as she and Dylan followed Ace.

"He's not finding anything," Dylan observed as Ace scurried from one leftover relic to another.

Beep beep beep. The detector emitted a solid stop-and-go sound that she recognized.

"It appears that I have, though." She bent her knees and pocketed a handful of pennies and dimes.

He shook his head and chuckled. "Is that penny-ante change even worth picking up?"

"It's the thrill of the treasure hunt. I've found plenty of cool stuff over the years—thimbles, eyeglasses, Confederate coins—but don't worry," she assured him. "I'm fully aware that we're searching for more grisly mementos today."

His eyes widened. "Actually, that's pretty cool. Any of it valuable?"

"Probably not. Whatever I've found in the

wildlife refuge, I've turned in. They're on exhibit in the park's visitor center."

They continued roaming, watching as Ace explored the oxidized steel frame, axles and fenders of an old car. The metal detector's continual hum was occasionally broken by choppy beeps as it scanned junk targets.

"How do you know it's not signaling something that might be useful?" Dylan asked.

"Years of experience. Asymmetrical objects like pull tabs from cans or iron objects make that noise. We're searching for jewelry. Specifically, a missing necklace and cross and a claddagh charm." She regarded him uneasily. "Do you think I'm wasting everyone's time, like Evan implied?"

"You have to admit it's a long shot. But a waste of time? No. If there's any possibility of finding one of the women or any clues about their fate, it's worth exploring."

Bailey let out a sigh, not even realizing until that moment that she'd been feeling so tense. If Evan had refused her request, she'd have searched alone during her off days. But searching now, with a cop, was way quicker and more efficient. Even if he wasn't the cop she'd have chosen to work with.

"Thank you," she murmured, oddly transfixed by his warm, understanding gaze. Her breath caught in her throat and her stomach gave an unfamiliar lurch as they stared at one another for several heartbeats.

Dylan abruptly whistled for Ace, and they set off down the dirt path that led to the Native American mound and, further down, to the forsaken site where the timber company had left its old equipment and the railroad tracks laid down to ship out the cypress. Lucky for her, Ace pretty much ignored them as he trotted several feet ahead, sniffing as he went.

The sun began to pummel them, and Bailey patted her face with a handkerchief.

"The heat's brutal," Dylan complained. "How do you stand it every day?"

"You get used to it."

He stopped and chugged half a bottle of water before calling Ace over. A small plastic cup in the evidence kit served as a makeshift bowl for the dog, who eagerly lapped up the water. Bailey watched, taking a judicious swig from the canteen she kept strapped on her shoulder. Dehydration was always a concern during the swamp summers.

"How much farther?" Dylan asked, putting the cup and empty bottle in a plastic bag.

"We're almost to the mound. Just around the next bend."

They resumed walking the road, which was

nearly grown over with trees and brush. She found her eyes drawn to Dylan several times, studying his features. In addition to the unusual eye color he shared with his father, there was something about his strong jaw and broad shoulders that resembled Armstrong Senior's. As far as temperament, Dylan had the same easy smile and sincere expression on his face. One that promised *you can talk to me* and *you're safe with me*.

All lies.

A sudden spurt of anger quickened her steps. Dylan upped his pace and shot her a quizzical glance.

"Something wrong?" he asked.

Bailey drew several deep breaths. Logically, she knew it was unfair to visit the sins of the father on the son, but the knot of resentment remained tight.

"Just eager to search the mound," she lied. Ignoring his skeptical frown, Bailey kept her eyes forward. "And here we are," she said, pointing at the hip-high mound.

"Easy to miss. It's even more overgrown than the time I came here on a field trip in junior high."

It was true. Marsh grass and saw palmetto covered the small mound. Dylan again had Ace sniff the cloth samples. As the dog began his search, Bailey turned on the metal detector and combed the area, small sections at a time.

"My office is going to furnish me with a detector tomorrow, so I can help you at the next location," he volunteered, walking around the perimeter of the mound.

"That'll save time."

Dylan pointed at a pair of dilapidated sheds nearby. "I'm going to take a quick look inside those."

She watched as he walked over, Ace following at his heels. He gestured for the dog to sit, then cautiously peered in the entrance of each shed.

Moments later he returned, shaking his head "no" at her questioning look.

She'd expected as much but was still disappointed. Bailey continued sweeping the mound until the machine's hum shifted to a beep. Her heart rate increased as she bent low to the ground, and then slowed as she eyed a half-dozen bobby pins, so rusted she almost feared she'd get tetanus by merely touching them.

"What do you have there?" Dylan crouched beside her.

"Probably nothing to get excited about. They most likely fell out of the hair of some long-ago tourist."

"I'll bag them up, just in case."

His bare forearm brushed hers, and she became hyperaware of his nearness, of his masculine scent of leather and sandalwood. Ace's body pushed between them, and she jumped to her feet with a startled gasp. Immediately, she cleared her throat in a belated attempt to cover the sound. Ace sniffed experimentally at the bobby pins, then meandered off.

"Since your dog had no reaction, those definitely didn't belong to the missing women, right?" asked Bailey.

"Seems unlikely," he agreed.

"I'll start checking the opposite end." Had she led them on a wild-goose chase after all?

Half an hour later, as she was almost ready to admit defeat, the metal detector emitted a strong beep. Bailey arced the tool, pinpointing the location, and sat on her haunches, trowel and probe in hand.

Dylan stepped in front of her, his tall figure providing a modicum of shade. Even Ace ran over, eager to be in on the action. "Let's see what you got there."

Bailey stopped and eyed the dog warily. Dylan snapped his fingers and pointed behind him. Ace obeyed the silent command, head down and issuing only a slight whimper of protest. The probe beeped again, revealing the hidden object's shallow depth.

Dylan handed her a pair of plastic gloves—

"Just in case," he murmured—and she donned them before carefully lifting a scoop of dirt and sifting through the clumps. Her fingers pressed against a hardened circular object. Possibly a pebble… No, its center was hollow. She finished brushing away the dirt and held it to the light.

A white-gold ring, its solitary diamond gleaming impossibly clear as she held it victoriously between them.

"Engagement ring?" Dylan suggested. "Heck of a place to lose it."

She opened her canteen and trickled water over the ring, then wiped it on her shirt until it shone. The ring was etched inside. "'Forever,'" she read. "'L.S. & R.K.'"

"Initials don't match our women," Dylan noted.

"True." Yet her skin felt tight all over. "How do you lose an engagement ring out here? It's not a campsite, no reason to ever take it off. This feels—" she mentally grasped for the right word "—deliberate."

Dylan shrugged as he dug out his cell phone. "Maybe someone recently divorced threw it away in a fit of disgust?"

The camera flash exploded, and she placed the ring in the evidence bag he held out. "You'll check it out, though, right?"

"That's why we're here," he said. "Are we finished with this mound?"

"As good as any one person can be with one metal detector. It's not much farther to the sheds."

"Good. Let's get a move on. We'll wrap it up here, then boat back to headquarters and grab a bite to eat. I want something more substantial than a sandwich. I'll email the photo to Jeff, a friend of mine in the office, and have him do a quick search on the ring. See if it has any significance in an ongoing investigation."

She couldn't ask for more than that. But the whole time they trekked to their next location, Bailey couldn't help feeling like everyone was merely humoring her wild whim.

Pride be damned. If nothing turned up, she'd at least tested her instincts. So what if Evan and a couple of people in the sheriff's office were secretly annoyed? She could live with that.

Ugly rusted machines sprung into their line of vision, jarring in the otherwise pristine wilderness. Railroad tracks lay twisted on the ground like iron snakes, weeds and marsh grass growing between the slats. All were relics from an ill-conceived attempt in the 1920s to conquer the swamp by draining it, selling its timber and shipping it out by rail.

The formidable Okefenokee Swamp had won

that battle, and the company had cut its losses and admitted defeat.

Ace ran to one of the two sheds at the edge of the site, both in serious disrepair, each precariously tilted to one side. They hurried to catch up with the beagle and entered the first shed. Stale, humid air hit Bailey, and she breathed deeper, trying to suck the oxygen out of the heaviness. Ace looked back from his sniffing, but Dylan stayed silent, and the dog returned to work, weaving a path to the right corner of the shed. It didn't take long till Ace pawed at the ground and barked—once, twice, three times. He'd found something.

Chapter Five

Dylan's throat went dry at the dog's signal.

He tried to quash the adrenaline of excitement spiking his blood. It could be a false alarm.

"Ace only has rudimentary training as a cadaver dog," he cautioned Bailey when she questioned him. He took out his cell phone and hurried to the corner. "Certified cadaver dogs go through eighteen months to two years of specialized training."

The dirt floor was packed solid except for Ace's recent pawing. No evidence of recent digging here. Yet Ace sat immobile, muscles tensed. Dylan snapped two quick photos and stuffed the cell phone back in his pocket.

"What do you believe your dog's found?" Bailey asked, rubbing her arms nervously. "Do you think…" Her voice trailed off as though too horrified to verbalize what they both wondered.

"Do I think someone's buried here? There's no evidence the earth's been recently disturbed, so it can't be the women we're searching for. It might not even be a body. But yeah, Ace has definitely found something."

Bailey licked her lips. "What's the next step?"

"We bring in a cadaver dog. If it finds human remains, then this place will be crawling with a team of forensic experts."

"I don't know whether I want them to find bodies or not," she admitted softly, her breath ghosting the side of his neck.

"Always better to know. For the sake of the victims' families and to catch the killer. We may have a serial killer on our hands. If we do, we've got to find him ASAP and prevent other deaths."

"Yes, of course."

"Let's not get ahead of ourselves," he cautioned. "We'll go back to town as planned and report our discoveries."

But Bailey stayed rooted, eyes focused on the hard patch of ground. "You don't think the two missing women are alive, do you?"

"No."

She finally faced him. "But you hear stories on the news about different guys kidnapping women and keeping them locked in a basement for years. Maybe our guy has them hidden away."

"Those are huge news stories because they're rare," he argued. "This situation is different. The wildlife refuge has no permanent residential housing. Even if he found a place to hide victims, he wouldn't have easy, constant access to them."

Her chin lifted. "He might still not want to kill them both straightaway. The guy might keep one or both around temporarily. It's only been two weeks."

He gazed into her hopeful, optimistic eyes, which weren't jaded from years of investigating brutal crimes. She wanted so badly to believe that those women were out there, alive and waiting for rescue. Much as he didn't want to destroy her hope, it would be cruel to encourage false optimism.

"We don't have concrete evidence yet that there's been foul play," he said. "Those women could have fallen out of their kayaks. We both know that can be deadly in these waters."

Alligator food. Bailey would get the point without him spelling it out so crudely.

Dylan whistled for Ace to follow him. The dog obeyed and slowly walked forward, occasionally craning his head backward, a barely audible mewl escaping his throat. Bailey gave Ace a wide berth and strode ahead of them. Outside, he drew a deep breath of fresh though sticky-hot air, glad to leave the sweltering shed behind.

The ride to headquarters was quiet, the boat puttering through the narrow water trails. The bit of breeze it created provided a welcome relief from the late-afternoon sun. Ace curled in his lap and fell asleep. Dylan rubbed him behind the ears, and Ace issued a contented moan without opening his eyes. "Good job today, boy," he murmured.

Bailey appeared absorbed in her thoughts, which was fine with him, as his own mind kept looping through the day's discoveries and what their implications might be.

Once in town, they agreed to eat at Fat Man's BBQ. On the shaded restaurant patio, they had the place practically to themselves. Dylan emailed the engagement ring photo to Sheriff Chesser, along with an account of the dog's possible find at the shed. Ace settled at his feet with a biscuit and bowl of water as they dug into their platters of pulled pork, beans and coleslaw.

"Anything for dessert?" the waitress asked as they finished their meal. "Got some homemade pecan pie this afternoon."

"I'm in. You?" he asked Bailey.

She nodded, and he almost wanted to applaud her for not remarking on the pie's gazillion calories. Not that she had anything to worry about. Her figure was lean and toned, no doubt aided by her vigorous outdoor job.

"What made you go into forestry?" he asked curiously. "Seems to be a field dominated by men."

She shrugged. "Can't imagine working in an

office. Being outside, mostly working alone, that's more my style."

"Those the only reasons?"

"It's peaceful."

He waited, but she didn't volunteer more information, so he prodded further. "Thought you'd mention saving the environment. I pictured you being into the whole conservation thing."

"'Course I am."

Again, she didn't elaborate, apparently content to dine in silence. "Are you always this quiet, or does something about me rub you the wrong way?"

"Yes."

Genuine confusion gusted through him. Bailey obviously wanted to avoid clarification. "Yes to what—both?"

The waitress returned to their table and set down two pie slices. Dylan pushed his aside as Bailey dug into hers.

"I'm solitary by nature," she said around a mouthful of food.

"I'm not talking about that part. I sense I'm not exactly your favorite person." Confusion gave way to irritation. "Why the attitude with me? I took your side this morning when your boss wavered on whether you should be included in a search."

"Let it go, okay? It'll make the rest of our work week go by more smoothly."

Sighing, he dug into his own pie. Did it really matter if she had some unknown grudge against him? Or maybe it wasn't him per se. Maybe…

"Did you or your family ever have some run-in with my dad?" he asked her.

That had happened to him a few times before. Once from Tommy Vaughn, a guy in high school whose father had been arrested for theft. Another time, nearly three years ago, from Vern Ashcroft, whom his dad had arrested for assault. In both cases, Tommy and Vern always treated him with a mixture of resentment and embarrassment.

"A run-in," she repeated slowly. "Yeah, you could say that."

He let the matter drop. First opportunity, he'd check the police computer database for an answer. Dylan slapped a credit card on the table when the waitress brought the bill. "My treat."

"I'll pay for my own." Bailey dug out her credit card and placed it next to his. He opened his mouth to remind her of their truce, but she spoke first. "It's getting too late for another excursion. We'll have to regroup in the morning."

"You got another place in mind?"

"Floyd's Island," she said immediately. "There's an old hunting cabin that could be used as a temporary shelter, and there's a huge Native American mound nearby as well."

"Even I've heard of that mound. The old timber company cut through a large portion of it to build a railroad." He rolled his eyes. "They claimed to have found giant-sized skeletons, which, conveniently, disintegrated almost immediately upon excavation."

"Such a skeptic," she said, her mouth twitching up at the corners—evidently unable to suppress her amusement. "Georgia's ancient race of giants. The tourists love that story. Too bad we don't have any giant bones in our little museum. Just the usual pottery and bead mound relics."

The waitress gathered their cards. "Be right back, sugar."

"Exactly how many isolated cabins and old mounds are there in this swamp?" he asked.

"Last count, there're seventy-four mounds in all."

He almost choked on his soda. "Surely you don't want to explore every last one of them?"

"Only those near old buildings." Bailey smirked and then added, "Lucky for us there aren't that many shelters left. Besides Floyd's, we could also explore Chesser Island. That should cover our bases."

"Okay, then. We can call it quits for now. I'll procure a metal detector, and early morning, we can meet at—" His cell phone rang, and he answered it with a grimace of apology to Bailey. "Armstrong here."

"Come down to the office. Right away." Sheriff Chesser's voice was tight with urgency.

"Sure. What's up? Did you get a hit on the ring?"

Bailey's eyes snapped to his, pie forgotten. She motioned to the waitress and quickly signed her bill.

"Yeah. It belonged to a Lisa Shaw, who disappeared just over four years ago. I'll give you more details once you get here."

"We're on our way."

Bailey shoved to her feet as he signed his own receipt. Ace sensed the excitement in the air and perked up from his nap, refreshed and curious.

She waited until they were in his car before asking, "Who did the ring belong to?"

"A woman who disappeared three years ago. Lisa Shaw. Does the name ring a bell with you?"

"No. You?"

"It's teasing the back of my brain, but I can't recollect why."

"Maybe Evan remembers her." She got out her cell phone to call, but he shook his head.

"Better wait and let the sheriff keep Evan informed."

She sighed and dropped the phone in her lap. "I hate all this chain-of-command bull."

Dylan didn't reply, yet he couldn't agree with her more. However, if they both wanted to remain on the case, then they had to follow protocol.

With light traffic, they were soon inside the busy sheriff's office, where noise from the jail, located at the back of the building, provided a constant background hum. They slipped inside Chesser's office, and he motioned for them to have a seat at his conference table, where he already had a laptop set up, its screen illuminated with an enlarged photo of the ring they'd found.

Chesser opened a file. "Lisa Shaw disappeared on April 16, 2016. She and her sister left Birmingham on a Thursday morning and traveled to Amelia Island for a weekend getaway. On Saturday morning, at approximately seven a.m., she told her sister she wanted to go on a boat tour of the Okefenokee. Her sister preferred to stay on the beach, so Lisa left on her own. She was never seen again."

Chesser took a photo from the file and slid it across the table to them. The woman looked to be in her midtwenties, blonde and smiling like the world was her oyster. Nothing like the two sisters who'd disappeared two weeks ago. Lisa was short and plump with carefully applied makeup, a lacy top and curled hair, while Mary Thornton and Amy Holley were both brunettes with the long, lean build of experienced kayakers. In the photos of the recent missing women, neither had worn makeup, and their hair had been pulled back into casual ponytails.

Was he wrong trying to draw comparisons among the women? Had they all met a similar fate from the same abductor?

"We've got a cadaver dog and his handler arriving in the morning from Atlanta," Chesser informed them. "If there's a body in that shed, it'll be a circus around here. Just like it was in the initial search for the missing women."

"Do you want us—" Dylan pointed between himself and Bailey "—to continue searching more locations or join in with other state and federal police when they arrive?"

"Maybe." Chesser cast a curious look at Bailey. "What made you want to search this particular locale?"

"I thought Evan had already explained my reasoning." Her arms were crossed in a defensive stance. So he wasn't the only one who drew Bailey's ire. Could it be all cops she disliked? Or maybe she had issues with men or even people in general.

"I'd like to hear it from you." Chesser paused. "If you don't mind."

The *don't mind* part was a polite euphemism for *that's an order.* He meant for her to explain her logic. Apparently Bailey came to the same conclusion.

"After finding the necklace at the labyrinth and the cots in the old church, it seemed possible to me that the women had been held there and that an abductor buried one of their necklaces in a spot that must hold a sort of ritualistic attraction. Based on that, I wondered if the women might still be alive and if he might be taking them from place to place in the swamp. Places that contain abandoned structures. Bonus points if there were an archaeological or mystical area nearby."

Dylan eyed her with renewed respect. Her theory was as good as anything else law enforcement had come up with. "Modern death artifacts mixed with ancient bones," he remarked.

Chesser and Bailey regarded him with reproach.

"Too early to say if anyone's been murdered," Chesser said. "We'll take matters day by day. Do you have other sites to visit?"

"Floyd's Island and then Chesser Island," Bailey informed him. "Chesser isn't as remote, so it's less likely to have been used." She regarded him curiously. "I take it you're descended from the original settlers?"

"There are dozens of us Chessers around the area," he confirmed. "Hearty progenitors, my folks. Had to be to arrive at a massive swamp and believe you can settle and conquer it."

Dylan had never heard him speak of his connections before, and the pride in his voice was evident. His boss turned to him. "Contact me as soon as you finish tomorrow. Anything special you require?"

"It would help to have a metal detector. Might make scanning an area easier and quicker."

"What about dogs? I can have Captain Woodard join you with more of them."

Bailey's back stiffened a degree.

"That's not necessary," Dylan said easily. "Ace is doing a great job all by himself. What we do need, though, is a cop to watch Ranger Covington's cabin this evening." Dylan quickly filled him in on the previous night's would-be arsonist.

Chesser's face darkened with concern, and he nodded. "Of course. Can't help but wonder if everything's connected. Hopefully we'll have answers soon. And if you change your mind about the dogs, just say the word."

"Thank you," Bailey said. "How much longer before forensics runs the test on the necklace we found yesterday?"

"They're short staffed and running behind but if a body is found, this matter will take precedence. There will be lots of public pressure to solve the case quickly."

"We could be dealing with a serial killer," Dylan said, verbalizing the elephant in the room.

The office went unnaturally quiet.

"One day at a time," Chesser reemphasized. He rose, signaling the meeting was over. "I'll give your boss a call and fill him in," he said to Bailey.

They exited his office and reentered the hum of the main room, where officers sat in cubicles. Jeff waved them over. "Where you been, man? Your sister's called three times already."

"Janie?"

"It's your niece's third birthday. Big party—" Jeff glanced at the clock hanging on the door across from them "—starting in about fifteen minutes."

Heck, it had completely slipped his mind.

"You go on," Bailey said. "I can catch a ride home with my neighbor."

"Why don't you come to the party with me? Plenty of cake and ice cream."

"No, thanks." With a small wave at Jeff, Bailey spun on her heels and started off.

"See you in the morning," Dylan called after her. He fought the urge to blow off the party and follow Bailey home. But Chesser had assigned an officer to watch her cabin that night. Surely she'd be okay between then and nightfall.

Jeff winked at him and lowered his voice. "Those legs. I remember her from the store years ago. She's still not impressed with you, dude."

"Give her time."

Despite the outward show of confidence, Dylan wasn't so sure.

"Better get a move on it. Janie's waiting," Jeff reminded him.

"Do me a favor. Run Bailey Covington's name in our system and see what shows up."

Jeff raised a brow. "That's highly irregular. Why?"

"Someone tried to hurt her last night. I want to know if there's anything in her background that would provide a clue as to who might have a motive. She did hint about a prior run-in with the law."

"Still waters run deep, huh?" Jeff rubbed his chin thoughtfully. "I'll call you later and fill you in."

Chapter Six

The scent of smoke and bacon wafted through the stagnant air as Bailey tied up their boat at Floyd's Island. Bright-colored kayaks in lime, red and yellow banked the shoreline.

"Still some campers around. Cooking breakfast before they shove off," she noted.

Her right shoulder ached as she lifted the metal detector onto the dock. Lugging around the machine for hours yesterday had taken a toll.

Dylan placed Ace on the dock and then gathered up his own supplies. Ace's toenails scrabbled across the old oak boards, and Bailey held her detector in front of her like a shield to prevent him from rubbing against her legs. On the boat ride, Dylan had kept him by his side, but the clever bugger was taking advantage of Dylan's momentary distraction to try to win her affection.

Bailey was having none of it.

"That bacon smells amazing," Dylan said as they walked onto land.

"Sure beats the trail mix we had for breakfast."

"Don't forget the cake."

They'd gotten up early enough without having to worry with cooking a meal. Instead, Dylan had arrived at her cabin with two huge slices of leftover birthday cake from his niece's party. She'd eagerly gobbled up the sweet treat. The handful of trail mix had been a guilty nod to ingest a bit of nutrition.

During the dawn boat ride, he'd regaled her with stories of his family—the cute niece, Laurie, who'd jumped up and down with joy at every present, his sister, Janie, who'd scolded him for arriving late, and his brother-in-law, Shawn, who was also one of his closest friends. Bailey suspected that his casual chatter was an attempt to lighten the mood of their potentially morbid search, but all the talk of family merely brought up buried resentments. She'd never had siblings or a father in her life. But that was bearable. Plenty of people grew up entirely well-adjusted without them. She and Mom had done fine until her mother was diagnosed with lung cancer and died less than six months later when Bailey was sixteen years old. With no living relative willing to take her in, Bailey had ended up in foster care. It had been a sad, scary time but what she couldn't bear was living with her foster father, Edgar Slacomb. The only blessing of that miserable period of her life was that it had lasted less than three years. But back then, each day had felt like a month. Every night, she'd mark off the completed day on her calendar with a thick black marker, gouging the innocent white square in much the way that she imagined inmates would cross off the days until reaching the end of their sentence.

Bailey strode quickly to the fire ring, inhaling the misty morning air, reminding herself that she was a free woman who refused to let the past define her present.

Two couples sat near the fire, sitting atop their neatly rolled sleeping bags, munching on bacon and toast. They hadn't booked the cabin so they must have slept on the ground. Their eyes rounded as they noted her ranger outfit and Dylan's cop uniform.

"Morning, Officers. Is there a problem?" asked one of the men, who shoved to his feet, brushing crumbs off his shorts.

One of the women grinned. "Y'all look like you're set for a treasure hunt."

Bailey acknowledged them with a quick nod, her stride to the cabin never slowing, as Dylan exchanged pleasantries with them and asked questions about how long they'd been in the area and if they'd witnessed anything unusual. Digging the key from her khaki shorts, she unlocked the cabin door and entered.

The spacious, four-room interior smelled faintly of lemon and cypress. It'd been cleaned only yesterday for visitors arriving later that afternoon. Built in 1925 as a hunting cabin, it was listed on the National Register of Historic Places and was a popular rental, even though hunting had been outlawed since the late 1930s. The gigantic stone fireplace gave it a cozy lodge feel, and she bet plenty of tall fish tales and hunting stories had been woven in that den.

Methodically she walked through every room, checking underneath cots and opening closets. Unless Ace was able to sniff out a trail, this could prove a wasted trip.

The front door squeaked open and then clattered shut. "Find anything out of place in here?" Dylan called.

"Nothing." She walked back to the den. "I checked the log earlier. It's been cleaned three times in the past two weeks for different renters."

"Ace still might be able to find a trace if the women were ever here. Isn't that right, boy?" Dylan patted the beagle before opening the bag holding the cloth samples from the missing women. Ace sniffed experimentally. "Go find," Dylan ordered.

The dog lowered his head and began his job.

Dylan, too, began a search, looking over what she'd already covered, opening cabinet drawers and lifting sofa cushions.

Bailey strode to the back window, staring at the woods, which formed a solid line only a few feet from the back wall of the house. It felt as though the woods were encroaching upon her, a smothering heaviness asserting its wild dominion over humans and the shelters they erected. Just as the ocean reclaimed inches of shoreline every year, the swamp also seemed to slowly swallow up islands of dry ground until one day, the land would completely disappear into the morass. She pictured the bodies of the missing women slowly sinking into quicksand, gobbled up inch by inch until only a few air bubbles marked their spot—and then that, too, vanished.

She shook off the depressing notion and returned to the task at hand. Until, or if, the bodies were found, there was always hope.

Had the abductor been bold enough to break and enter a cabin popular with renters? If so, he'd taken a substantial risk. Maybe that was part of the thrill for him, though. Pushing the limits in his own arrogance, always believing he could stay a step ahead of the law. Good. The more the man imagined his crime trail invincible, the sooner he'd slip and leave behind a vital clue.

"We've got nothing," Dylan announced at last.

"Is it even worth checking out the mound, then?"

He shrugged. "Might as well while we're here. Floyd's the largest island in the Okefenokee. Maybe ruling it out is at least a step in the right direction. Narrows the search a bit."

With lower spirits than when they'd arrived, they hiked to the mound just as the kayakers shoved off into the water trail.

The half-moon-shaped mound was several feet higher than the one at Billy's and desecrated by a swath cut from the old lumber company. Evidently in that era, people had no respect for preserving the sacred heritage and artifacts left behind by past civilizations.

Bailey retreated to one end of the mound, Dylan the other, slowly canvassing the area until they met in the middle. Ace did his usual thing, and Bailey was relieved by his total focus on the search. He wouldn't try to make friends with her while so absorbed.

Two hours later, the search ended. Dylan held up the evidence bag to the light—a broken necklace chain, three mismatched earrings and a rusted brooch. Ace gave the items a dismissive sniff.

"Doesn't look too promising," Dylan said.

She rubbed the back of her clammy neck and sighed. "Wild-goose chase."

"We haven't searched the cabin grounds yet."

Bailey took a swig from her canteen before nodding briskly. "Guess we should get to it."

"I have a better idea. We need a break. Let's motor over to Billy's Island and see what they've uncovered before heading to town. We'll turn in this bag at the office—" he held up their meager findings "—and then we can have a long lunch and return to Floyd's late afternoon when it's not so hot."

Even though she was acclimated to the heat, the idea of resting sounded too good to pass up. And she was more than a little curious if anything had been discovered at yesterday's site. "I've been thinking about their dig all morning," she admitted.

"Me, too."

Bailey pointed to the two-way radio hitched at his belt. "They haven't told you anything?"

"We're out of radio range. Lost it about a mile and a half before landing at the dock."

They made their way back to the boat, and she imagined the scene they'd find at Billy's, men with shovels, chipping away at the ground in search of grisly human remains. Not the kind of job she'd ever relish, but she had tremendous respect for the trainers and dogs who performed the task.

The boat motor whirred to life, and she navigated onto the waterway, glad for the wind against her face. Even Ace appeared tuckered out. After lapping up a bowl of water, he snuggled against Dylan's feet and immediately lapsed into a deep sleep, complete with loud snores and grunts.

If only she could fall into sleep so effortlessly. The past night, she'd tossed and turned more than she'd slept, remembering that an unknown person had tried to douse her cabin with gasoline. Could the abductor have figured out her identity so easily? Or was it someone else entirely? A chill ran up her spine as her mind focused on a potential suspect.

"What are you thinking about?" Dylan asked.

She gave a start, flushing as she met his curious gaze. No sense in withholding the truth. "Wondering who poured gasoline around my cabin. I'll sleep better once they've been arrested."

"Still no idea who it could have been?"

She hesitated a heartbeat. "Not really."

Dylan's eyes tightened. "But you have a suspicion."

The man was far too observant. "It's farfetched. Crazy, really."

"Lay it on me."

"I'd rather not. I can't go around accusing someone with no evidence to back it up."

"Come on, tell me."

She could see he wasn't going to let it go. Bailey navigated the boat around a fallen tree, not wanting to face him as she explained. "It's just... I'm not on good terms with the foster family I lived with in high school. Especially the man."

She couldn't—wouldn't—call him *father*.

"I see."

She darted him a quick glance, relieved to see on his face calm acceptance and not the pitying look she so despised when she'd discussed her background with others. Not that she ever much did. Even Lulu only knew a few bits and pieces from that miserable period of her life.

"It's stupid to point a finger. It was a long time ago. No reason for him to suddenly stalk me or try to hurt me—" *again*, she added mentally "—after all these years."

"He still live near here?"

"Not far. In Waycross." The larger town, with a separate park entrance, was about thirty miles west of Folkston.

"What's his name?"

"Doesn't matter."

"Come on. I'll check him out. I can at least eliminate him as a suspect if he has a solid alibi for the last few days."

Right. Like she'd ever trust an Armstrong again.

"The time for police help with that creep has

long gone by. Besides, if he still means me harm, he's had plenty of opportunity to hunt me down over the years." The words soured her throat. Even she could hear the scalding bitterness in her voice.

"I see," he said again.

"You see nothing."

"What's that supposed to mean?"

"Not a thing. Forget it."

"Heck, no, I'm not forgetting it."

Silence stretched between them, broken only by the boat motor and the chatter of birds and insects.

"Bailey," he said softly. "Look at me."

She did. And the compassion in his olive eyes made her breath catch.

"Sounds like your foster father was a real piece of work. I wish someone had intervened on your behalf. A cop, a teacher, a friend. Anybody."

"Hard to make friends when you aren't allowed to socialize with anyone your own age. And confiding to a teacher was out. They homeschooled me."

Dylan winced. "I'm sorry. So they kept you isolated, which is typical with abusers. Wasn't there someone you could have reached out to? A social worker? The police?"

"Oh, I reached out, all right." Dylan opened

his mouth to ask the obvious question, but she rushed to distract him. "Why are you so curious? Do you think he might be the arsonist?"

"We should take a hard look at anyone with a violent history. Thought we had already done that, actually. And if he's capable of setting your cabin on fire while you were asleep inside, maybe he's capable of these other crimes as well. I wouldn't rule him out."

Edgar, a killer? Bailey mulled over the possibility. Had he graduated from abusing foster kids to the crime of kidnapping, and perhaps even murder? Somehow, she couldn't picture him doing it. The man was too stupid and too lazy to stalk women in the wilderness and then manage to elude police. But setting fire to her cabin? She could believe that.

"I don't believe he's our guy. He's more of an opportunist," she said slowly. "Younger victims and easy access to them is more his style."

Dylan frowned. "He's not still fostering children, is he?"

"No. I turned him in as soon as I moved away. My report, along with social worker suspicions on a girl who lived there after me, got him and his wife removed from the foster care system."

"Glad for that, at least. Hope you pressed charges."

"I didn't. But he can't ever foster more children, and I'm good with that."

"So he doesn't have a record, then."

"Never got caught committing a crime that I'm aware of."

At the sharp bend in the water, their boat suddenly sidled alongside an alligator basking in the sun. It hissed at them and slunk away into the marsh grass.

"Sorry, Gimpy," she called out. "Wasn't paying attention there."

"Gimpy?"

"He only has three legs. We suspect a turtle feasted on the missing one."

His brows rose, and his lips twitched in amusement. "You actually name these gators?"

"Yep," she said, relieved to note that Dylan was distracted from their earlier conversation. "There's Big Momma, Burt, Bessie, and the one that hangs out by the mouth of this trail is called Gatekeeper. He keeps a close guard on his territory."

"So, we humans are merely visitors here?"

"Absolutely. Bears and gators rule this swamp."

Dylan rubbed his chin, gazing out at the water prairie of lily pads and cypress. "I know they're shy of humans, and there's never been a case of a gator attack out here, but if they came across a dead body dumped overboard by a killer…"

"Not their preference, but food is food."

Only the sound of the boat motor broke the hum of swarming insects and chirping birds as they both chewed over the reminder that one or both of the missing women might be cached below the tannin-stained water, reduced to a mere alligator feast.

At last, they banked on Billy's Island, where several boats had docked. Uniforms were everywhere, swarming around the dilapidated shed, shovels in hand. Ace barked, his dark brown eyes alight with excitement. He started to trot ahead, but Dylan called him back to his side.

"Does this mean…" Her voice trailed off, unable to say the words.

"Probably." His face was grim as they strode over to the group of cops.

Bailey hardly knew what to hope for. She desperately didn't want to think of anyone buried in the wilderness, but if they were dead, then finding the bodies was the best thing for their grieving families.

The stench hit her before she was even close enough for an update, a thick wall of putrefaction stronger than anything she'd ever experienced, powerful enough to make her eyes water and her lungs choke. She'd never been exposed to a rotting corpse before, but no one had to tell her what had been dug up in that old shed.

She knew.

Chapter Seven

Dylan cast a worried look at Bailey. Even for seasoned law enforcement officers this was a grisly, disturbing scene. He tried to shield her view when several men lifted a plastic body bag to carry to an awaiting boat. But Bailey stoically stood her ground and took in everything, even if her face had paled and there was a slight tremble in her hands.

Dylan spoke to one of the officers and learned that the body was female and had been buried for several years.

"We should return to work," Bailey said, heading back to their boat.

"I think we've done enough for the day," he said, but she ignored him.

Resignedly, Dylan sprayed his arms and neck with insecticide. It felt like saturating his body with poison, but if he didn't want to get chewed up by swarming yellow flies, he had no option.

The sun set low, and he'd tried to dissuade Bailey from returning to Floyd's Island, but she'd insisted they complete their search of the cabin grounds before calling today's effort a total loss. Tomorrow, they'd regroup and decide where to go next.

"Waiting one more day to search isn't critical. After finding that body, we'll probably be flooded with more cops and volunteers, starting tomorrow morning," he said. "It's not all on us."

"Good. We could use their help."

He tried to adopt her pragmatic attitude. Privately, he found all the extra help annoying, as state and federal cops homed in on his territory and acted as though they possessed superior intelligence and skill. He might be employed in a rural county sheriff's office, but he and his co-workers knew this land and the local swampers better than any outsider.

They left the metal detectors on the boat and headed toward the cabin. The machines wouldn't be needed unless they discovered something of a suspicious nature that warranted a closer look.

At the cabin's rear, Ace perked up, yipping in high-pitched squeals. Dylan exchanged a quick, surprised glance with Bailey, and then they hurried to catch up to the dog. On the back porch, Ace paced the old wooden boards, a whimper warbling through his chest before he stopped in front of a weathered kindling box and gave three deep barks.

Quickly, they both donned plastic gloves and carefully climbed the rotting porch steps. After a snapshot on his cell phone, Dylan moved the box aside.

Nothing. His shoulders rounded in disappointment.

No, wait—did that pattern of chicken scratching in the wood mean anything? He bent closer, using the cell phone as a flashlight.

The letters *A M* were gouged in the rotten wood.

Short for Amy? The missing Amy Holley? More scratchings were below the letters, and he squinted, trying to decipher their meaning. Bailey took his arm, directing the light beam further up and to the left at another etched marking.

H E L P

He sucked in his breath.

"She's alive!" Bailey swiveled her head toward the forest as though expecting Amy Holley to materialize from its dark depths.

"At some point she was, yes," he cautioned. "Doesn't mean she still is."

"What else did she write?"

He studied the floorboard, unsure how to decipher the crude, irregular markings. "Looks like she tried to make a circle with some kind of drawing inside of it."

"A tree?" Bailey suggested, cocking her head to one side as she gazed intently down.

"Maybe?" But it was a guess. "What did she use to write with?" he muttered, then glanced around, spotting a sharp rock nearby. "Aha," he breathed, gathering it into a baggie.

"Great. Her prints should be all over that," Bailey said.

She had been right after all. Until a dead body was found, there was hope. Whoever held Amy against her will hadn't killed her immediately.

Ace growled, and Bailey suddenly jumped to her feet. "Did you hear something?"

He scrambled to his feet as well, hand automatically traveling to his sidearm. Dylan shielded her with his body, scanning the woods in all directions for signs of movement. Ace continued growling, baring his fangs at an unknown menace. "What did you hear?"

"A rustling behind us. Could have been a deer," she offered skeptically.

This was supposed to be only a search for clues, not a cat-and-mouse game with a killer. He needed backup, and there was no way to radio for help. They were sitting ducks, an open target, for whoever was out there, watching, maybe even taking aim at them.

A whistling buzzed near his ear, and Dylan threw his body over Bailey, knocking them both to the ground. An explosion sounded above them, and wood shards rained down. Ace charged off the porch.

"Crawl to the side of the cabin and make a run for the boat," he breathed into Bailey's ear.

"But what about—"

"Just do it. I've got your back. Get in the boat, head back and radio for help."

Bailey crawled away, and he followed, gun raised. She dropped to her feet at the edge of the porch. "What about you?"

"I'll hold him off. Go on."

She glanced at him doubtfully as another shot rang out.

"You're my best hope," he told her, knowing it was the only thing he could say to get her to leave him.

With a reluctant nod, she took off running.

Dylan crouched by the side of the porch steps and discharged his weapon in the direction from which the shots had been fired. Little chance his bullet would hit the attacker, but he wanted to demonstrate he had his own firepower. He'd put up a fight.

"Get back," Dylan ordered Ace.

But the beagle was having none of it. He

stopped running, though, and began barking furiously, eyes and ears focused on the woods.

Another shot rang out, and Ace fell to the ground with a sharp yelp of pain. The sound filled Dylan with fury.

"This is the police! Give yourself up!" he shouted.

In response, yet another round exploded, hitting the porch railing only inches from where he crouched.

His ears strained in the ensuing silence. Why hadn't he heard the boat motor?

The ominous quiet settled, thick and cloying, grating on his nerves. At least with gunshots firing, he had an idea where the shooter was. But now? He could be anywhere, sneaking up on him from any direction. Ace whimpered and limped to him. Blood trickled down his right haunch.

Dylan scooped Ace into his arms, rose up a couple of feet and made a run for the front of the cabin. A shot exploded in the gathering twilight, and he braced, expecting to feel searing pain. Grateful he didn't, he reached the front of the cabin, where Bailey ran toward him.

"Fuel line's cut," she called out breathlessly. "We're stuck."

They were so screwed.

"Get in the cabin!" he ordered.

Bailey held up the keys, already one step

ahead of him. He covered her back, gun at the ready, as she undid the lock.

"Backup's on the way!" he yelled into the darkness. "Don't be stupid. Drop your gun and step forward with your hands in the air."

The door creaked open, and they quickly stumbled inside.

"Run to the hallway," he told Bailey. There were no windows there, and she'd be safe for the time being. Dylan locked the door and assessed the layout. The two largest windows faced the front and back of the cabin, but there were also two small side windows.

"I'll keep watch at the back while you watch the front," Bailey volunteered.

"You're not armed. Just get in the hallway."

She didn't bother answering, and she didn't move from her position flattened on the wall next to the back window.

He quickly turned his gaze to the front and watched the lengthening shadows darken in the swampy gloom. Four shots had been fired. Which meant their attacker had at least two left. Just enough to kill them both.

An eerie cacophony of pig frogs, cicadas and God-knew-what-else began their night songs. His eyes and ears strained, trying to pick out the tiniest rustle or shifting of moonlight in the darkness. He heard a roaring sound and started, until he realized it was only the pounding of his blood in his ears.

Ace gave a low moan, laying his head on Dylan's right shoe. Poor guy. The dog needed a medal if they came out of this alive.

Time slowed, the night growing impossibly darker by the second. How long had they been standing there, poised for disaster? Could be sixty seconds, could be an hour.

"I think he's gone," Bailey said softly. He could barely discern her silhouette in the short distance between them.

Why hadn't their attacker taken another shot? Maybe the guy was used to controlling vulnerable civilians and not exchanging potshots with an officer of the law. Or maybe he'd believed the lie about backup arriving at any moment.

"Gone where?" he asked. "He's out there somewhere under cover of darkness. Watching and waiting."

"It's past time for me to check in for the end of my shift. Evan knows we're here at Floyd's. He'll come."

"Ditto. Chesser will raise an alarm as well."

"Evan warned me I was cutting it close time-wise, coming out so late in the day." Her voice was flat and heavy.

"I take responsibility for that. It was my idea to check at Billy's and then break for lunch."

"No, I'm the one who insisted we return."

Not that it mattered. They were a team. "Guess neither of our bosses is going to be too happy about a night rescue operation."

"What if—" She hesitated. "What if our rescuers walk into a trap? There's no way to warn them about the shooter."

"Don't worry. They'll be prepared for the worst."

Ace gave a louder whimper.

"How badly is your dog hurt?" Bailey asked.

"Appears to be a flesh wound, though it's bound to hurt like heck."

The whir of a motor broke into the background drone of the swamp's night creatures.

"Have they come for us already?" Bailey asked doubtfully. "Or is that our attacker escaping?"

"Either way, it's good news for us."

He waited, eyes focused forward, straining to see if anyone approached. There were no lights, no shouts, no one calling their names.

"Pretty sure it's our guy slipping away," Dylan said at last. "Too soon for the others to have raised the alarm and made their way over. We might as well have a seat and wait for them. Let's go over here," he directed, walking to one corner of the den. "We'll sit together facing outward, and if anyone comes in unannounced, I'll have us covered."

Awkwardly they settled on the floorboards. Ace scrabbled to join them, then plopped down between them with a whine. Dylan felt Bailey stiffen beside him, and he reached to move Ace to his other side, but she crisply said, "Leave him be."

His hand paused. "You sure?"

"He's injured. Shifting him will cause more pain."

As though sensing Bailey had made a concession on his behalf, Ace plopped his head on her knee and licked her skin.

Bailey flinched, then let out a rush of breath. "Yeah, yeah. Don't get used to it, buddy," she said gruffly.

He licked again, and that time, she accepted the overture, if not warmly, at least stoically.

Ace was definitely making headway in his campaign to win Bailey over. Day two, round two went to the dog. His money was on Ace for the eventual win.

"How soon will the body at Billy's be identified?" she asked.

"Should be an easy match, what with the teeth and skeleton all in one place."

"I'm afraid it's going to be Lisa Shaw."

"Me, too. It's the first record they'll check." He turned to her in the thick darkness. "Thanks to you. Your idea to search for trophies in a specific location might be the break we need to find our guy. He's certainly getting nervous. Tonight's attack proves it."

"I'm going to ask Evan if we can ban camping and outdoor activities in the swamp for all civilians until we catch the killer."

"He won't like that. Neither will local businesses that profit from the tourism."

"Evan can at least ban overnight excursions and issue a public warning to day visitors."

"Don't worry. Once news gets out that a body was found, which has probably already happened, it'll deter outdoor enthusiasts."

"Good."

They lapsed into silence, and he was intensely aware of her warm breath and the brush of her forearms against his, hot and sweet and intimate. She stretched out her legs—those long, lean legs that he never tired of seeing. Heck, he hadn't even known he was a leg man until he met Bailey. Absently he brushed his fingers over Ace's head. The dog was napping, a good sign that the pain had eased. A sudden thought had him frowning.

"You really plan on returning to your cabin this evening? Not sure that's wise."

"I'll be fine. Don't sleep outside my place in your truck again. We'll need a good night's rest to maintain our energy and focus tomorrow."

"Will you at least consent to an officer providing drive-by patrol again?"

"That works."

So, she just didn't want *him*. "Hey, while we're stuck here, mind filling me in on whatever grudge you have against me?"

His words weighted the air, and he watched her fingers tap against her thighs in a dance of suppressed agitation. Just when he gave up hope of her responding, Bailey let out a long sigh.

"It's nothing you've done. I shouldn't hold it against you."

"Hold what against me?"

"I did reach out a long time ago about my foster father. To a cop."

Outrage washed over Dylan. "And he didn't intervene?"

"Nope."

No wonder she had no love for law enforcement. "He should have. We're here to protect the vulnerable. There's no excuse for his behavior. Who was it?"

She shook her head. "He's no longer on the force."

"That's good, at least." Probably some temporary officer who wasn't fit for the job and either quit or got fired. He wondered if it was anyone he might have known. Off the force or not, he'd love to rip into the jerk. "I'd still like to know his name, though."

"Let it go. I have, or I'm trying to, anyway."

Dylan swallowed hard. "How bad was the abuse, Bailey?"

Again, she paused so long he didn't believe she'd answer.

"Never mind, it's—"

"A few beatings," she said, interrupting him. "It was a long time ago. I'm over it." Her shoulders rose in a dismissive shrug, but her effort to minimize the horror didn't fool him.

He inched a hand over and laid it on top of her fidgeting fingers. "I'm sorry for what you went through," he said simply.

Her body became as hard and unyielding as a statue. Had he made a mistake touching her? Moments passed, but instead of withdrawing, she turned her hand over and squeezed his fingers. The silent acknowledgment eased the underlying tension that had bubbled between them from the start. Here, under the cover of ink-black darkness, she'd bared a little of her soul, and it humbled him.

Ace's muscles violently twitched in the throes of some dream, and he jerked to a sudden awakening. His warm tongue lapped at their linked hands, and Bailey withdrew from his grasp, easing away to put a few inches between their bodies.

While she was in such a mellow mood, Dylan

decided to push his luck with one more question. "Why are you so afraid of dogs?"

Her mouth snapped open, so quick he knew it was a knee-jerk defensive response.

"It's okay. Nothing to be embarrassed about. You're certainly not the only person who fears them."

Bailey stood and strode to the front window, flattening her body against the wall before venturing a peek outside. "Let's just say I have a healthy respect for their bite."

"Because you were bitten?"

"Hmm. Still no sign of rescue," she commented.

He let it drop. Enough true confessions for one evening.

"Shouldn't be too much longer. It'll take about an hour for them to get here once they realize we never returned."

"Less than that. Evan will use the airboat. That should cut at least twenty minutes from the trip."

"Airboat?" He perked up. "You have an airboat? Why haven't we been using it? Geez, it could have saved us a ton of time."

"It's only for emergencies."

"Why?"

"It's bad for the environment and the wildlife."

"Yeah, well, isn't our search an emergency?" he grumbled.

"In the beginning, but not after the initial search was called off. Everyone gave up hope."

"And now we have leads. I'll have my boss speak to yours about getting us that airboat." A steady rumbling sounded from afar, and Dylan scrambled to his feet as Ace growled. "Don't step outside until we know for sure who's out there."

But Bailey was already halfway to the door. "I can tell from the sound that it's the airboat. Which means Evan's driving, and we're safe."

"We're not safe." Dylan hurried to the door and blocked her exit. "It's a long shot, but our attacker might still be in hiding. Ready to pick us off one by one."

"Then I have to warn them of the danger."

"Chesser's with Evan and I'd bet at least a couple more officers. He'll caution everyone to be on their guard."

They faced off in the stale opaqueness of the cabin, their breath mingling. A flush of heat scoured him as he absorbed the tingling nearness of her body so close to his own. She was affected, too. He could feel it in her sudden stillness and quickened breath.

Light flashed through the grimy windowpane, breaking the spell. Now that their rescuers were closer, he could make out the distinct sound of at least three different boat motors.

Help had arrived en masse.

Footsteps pounded on the boat dock, and floodlights lit the cabin. Chesser's voice abruptly boomed over a megaphone: "This is the police! Come out with your hands up."

Bailey raised a brow. "*Now* can we go?" Without waiting for an answer, she pointed at Ace. "Might have to carry him out."

He whistled, and Ace slowly limped to his side. Dylan scooped him into his arms, careful not to touch his wound. "Me first in case anyone is excessively trigger-happy," he said. "And be sure to keep your hands raised when you exit."

He ignored her exaggerated sigh and cautiously opened the front door, one hand behind his head, the other holding Ace. "Officer Armstrong," he called, stepping out. "Ranger Covington is right behind me."

The beam of a floodlight pierced his eyes, and he squinted at the dark, murky shadows of the officers. Someone barked out an order to cover all sides, and feet shuffled as officers formed a U-shape to defend themselves from every angle. Evidently, they were taking no chances that he and Bailey weren't in extreme danger. Dylan imagined this was what it felt like being rescued in a jungle during a covert military operation gone wrong.

"Are you two alone?" Chesser's voice still boomed over a megaphone, but he was much closer.

"Far as we know," Dylan called out. "We were attacked but believe he's left the area."

"Bailey, are you okay?"

He recognized Evan's voice.

"I'm fine," she called.

A dark figure emerged from the cluster of rescue workers, and Evan swiftly stepped forward and draped an arm over Bailey's shoulder. "You sure you're okay?" he asked gruffly.

A swift bolt of irritation crackled down Dylan's spine. Was Bailey's boss a little too touchy-feely with his employee, or was he imagining it? He'd taken an instant, irrational dislike of the man from the start, so perhaps he was reading too much into what was, after all, merely a side-armed hug.

He quickly filled the sheriff in on what had transpired as the officers made their way to the boat dock.

"We're closing in on him," Chesser noted with grim satisfaction. "First thing in the morning, I'll send Jeff and another officer to gather the spent shells and run ballistics tests. By then I hope we'll also know the identity of the body we dug up."

From the corner of his eyes, Dylan watched Evan, still with an arm over Bailey's shoulder, guide her to the airboat. His proprietary manner annoyed the heck out of Dylan, but for now, he'd let it go. He got in Chesser's boat.

The trek back to the park entrance was noisy as everyone chatted all at once about the day's discoveries and offered theories about the possible killer.

Alligator eyes glowed red whenever boat lights hit them on the water. Startling how prevalent they were as they slithered through the murk at night, hunting their prey. Was their killer also out there, eyeing them from a safe perch?

When Dylan's boat arrived at the park marina, Bailey and Evan were already there, waiting. "When and where are we meeting in the morning?" she asked him as he stepped onto the dock.

"Let's meet at the sheriff's office. Come as soon as you can. I'll be there."

"Shouldn't we take Ace to a vet first?"

"I'll have one of the K-9 officers take him immediately," Chesser volunteered. "If the vet doesn't keep him overnight, he'll be fine in our kennel."

"Kennel?" she asked, rounding on Dylan. "I thought he lived with you."

"No. Never has."

"You mean you work with this dog and then let him be shut in a kennel all night?"

"He's always lived like that. He's used to it."

Her lips pursed in an angry line. "Ace can stay with me if he doesn't need to stay with the vet. He can alert me in case of an intruder."

"That isn't necessary since you're—" He bit his tongue before saying the words *afraid of dogs*. "Like we discussed, you'll have a drive-by patrol this evening keeping watch on your cabin. You don't need Ace."

"He doesn't deserve to be alone all evening."

Her insistence surprised Dylan. Clearly, compassion won out over her fear.

"I want to do this," she said quietly. "He and I will get along just fine by ourselves."

Brave words. But Dylan suspected that what he had in mind for their work the next day would require every bit of her fortitude, and then some. Truth be told, she'd probably rather face their mysterious killer than what he had planned.

Chapter Eight

Despite the early hour, the sheriff's office was abuzz when Bailey entered the crowded room. From the litter of coffee cups and empty fast-food wrappers, she suspected that many of the officers had pulled an all-nighter. They were huddled around a massive whiteboard with black chunks of text and photos, like honeybees swarming a gallberry bush. Her eyes immediately caught Dylan's, and he rose from the massive conference table.

She walked closer to the board, curious about the suspects and theories. Bubbly smiles radiated from a photo of Mary Thornton and Amy Holley as they stood by their kayaks, ready to embark on a new adventure. Underneath were the names of their husbands with question marks—she supposed the closest of kin were always suspects—and then a list of all the employees of the adventure outfitter company. She scanned the names, then stopped at a familiar one: *Clay*

Slacomb. Blood pounded in her ears, and she bit the inside of her lip to ground herself.

There was only one name worse than Armstrong, and that was Slacomb.

"Everything okay?" Dylan murmured beside her.

Without replying, she abruptly exited, and he followed her into the hallway. Out of the group's earshot, Bailey rounded on him. "Tell me about Clay Slacomb. Has he been questioned?"

"Slacomb." Dylan rubbed his chin. "The outfitter employee? Yeah, they all were questioned, but nothing stood out with any of them. Why?"

"Interrogate him again."

His eyes sharpened. "What makes you suspicious of this guy?"

She disliked discussing her past, but she couldn't keep silent. "That abusive foster father I mentioned yesterday? Clay is his brother."

Dylan's face set in hard, determined lines. "Has Clay ever laid a hand on you?" he asked. His eyes had turned hard and cold, and his voice was the aural equivalent of sharp, pointy icicles.

She drew a shaky breath and fought back the ridiculous twinge of shame. "No, but he witnessed the abuse firsthand and he…laughed. Someone like that, well, I wouldn't put anything past him."

He reached a hand out as if to touch her, then

dropped it back by his side. "I want the name of Clay's brother, too."

"Edgar. Surely you don't think they acted together?"

"We can't rule anything out. Given their history, though, I'd put either one of them at the top of the suspect list. Listen, Bailey, I'd wanted us to question your foster father today, but if you'd rather not be present, I'll certainly understand."

See Edgar again? Her throat tightened as she pictured his angry, pinched face. The man had always acted ticked off at the world, ready for the tiniest provocation—one wrong word, one microexpression of disrespect on anyone's face— to detonate his temper. His brother was cut from the same cloth. The pair of them acted as though everyone had cheated them out of what they were entitled to—and they were determined to make everyone pay for that transgression.

"I'll go with you," she said flatly.

"You don't have to. Take the morning off, and I'll come pick you up when I'm done."

"No, I'm going, and that's that."

Dylan slowly nodded. "If you're sure."

"I am. And you'd better have another officer question Clay while we're speaking with Edgar. If not, he'll warn his brother of our suspicions. We don't want to give Clay time to prepare. Or possibly flee."

"Gotcha. Be right back."

Alone in the empty hallway, she shivered and rubbed her arms. How would Edgar react when he saw her after all those years? Was he still furious at her for filing a report against him? Stupid question. Of course he was. Nobody could hold a grudge like a Slacomb. For over a year after she'd left his house and spoken against him to a social worker, she'd received late-night phone calls. He'd called her a worthless fool, promising that she'd pay for her lies. When she'd threatened to file a restraining order against him, he'd finally stopped. Since then, she'd had no contact. Occasionally, in town, she'd see him or his wife, but she'd turn her back on them and avoid eye contact.

"Ready?" Dylan returned to her side, and they marched to his patrol car. "Where does he work?" he asked. "Think he'll be there or at home?"

She gave a derisive laugh. "He's too antisocial to actually hold a job. That would entail working alongside other people and reporting to a boss. No, he supposedly works from home. Runs an auto repair business out of his garage, but his place is so remote he doesn't get much business."

"And where's home?"

She gave him the address, and they slipped into silence as they left downtown Folkston and headed toward Waycross. Near the town limits, they turned off onto a dirt road, and then soon spotted the sprawling ranch home and the property that she'd vowed never to set foot on again.

So much for famous last words.

A pack of Dobermans stormed toward their car, barking furiously.

Her throat went dry, and her fingers dug into the door handle. "Watch out for the dogs. They're vicious. He lets them roam unless someone's booked an appointment at his shop."

Dylan popped open the glove compartment. "Grab a can of mace. If he doesn't control his dogs, I'll shoot them if they move to attack."

"Oh, they'll attack all right. That's what he's trained them to do." Wherever the pack roamed, Edgar was sure to be nearby. Her eyes scanned the property.

A figure stood in front of an open shed, clad in a white sleeveless T-shirt and baggy jeans streaked with grease. A cigarette—unfiltered and hand rolled—dangled from his thin lips. He squinted at them as he ran a hand through his thinning brown hair, which had more silver in it now than when she'd seen him last.

A cop car pulling up at his house was probably the most unwelcome sight Edgar could imagine—until he spotted her stepping out of the vehicle. Bailey surmised that he didn't want to see the likes of the woman who'd put a stop to his gravy-train foster care money. Not that the system provided much in the way of compensation, but he'd pocketed it all and in return provided only a closet-sized room and meals of peanut butter sandwiches. He and his wife, Millie, needed the money since his mechanic business was slow. Edgar was great at fixing vehicles, but he lacked customer relation skills. Which was to say, he ripped them off as much as he thought he could get away with, all the time sporting a smirk that did nothing to endear him for future business.

"Last chance to change your mind," Dylan said.

"No way." To her surprise, she found herself actually looking forward to this confrontation. Edgar wasn't so scary when he was outnumbered and in the presence of an armed officer. Her hand instinctively strayed to her necklace, and she stroked the soft crow feather. *Courage.* The cool, hard obsidian arrowhead lay heavy on her breastbone. *Power.*

The Dobermans surrounded the car, jumping up on the passenger doors, their nails scraping metal. Their pointy faces snarled by the windows. Her fingers curled into her palms. She'd rather face ten Edgars than one of those beasts.

"What the heck," Dylan muttered.

"He always keeps a pack. Trains them to attack at his command. And trespassers are always fair game."

"That him standing over there?"

She nodded, and Dylan lifted a megaphone to his mouth. "Call off your dogs, or I'll shoot them."

Edgar scowled and barked an order for them to "git." They retreated a few feet, bodies taut and mouths snapping as she and Dylan stepped out of the car. Bailey gripped the mace can tightly. Too bad she hadn't had it years ago when Edgar had sicced the pack on her. Good thing Ace was still at the vet that morning. These Dobermans would have chewed him up as an appetizer.

"Cage your animals," Dylan ordered. "Immediately."

Edgar scowled but ordered the dogs to the house. Millie magically appeared at the door and ushered them in. She was still a mousy brown ghost existing in the shadows, obeying Edgar's every command. Bailey almost felt sorry for her. *Almost.* But the woman had certainly never spared her any mercy during her time in that house. A bit of the tension in her belly unfurled as the last of the dogs entered the house and the door closed behind them.

"Whatcha want with me?" Edgar asked in gravelly, abrupt tones. Even his voice was mean, hard and damaged by a two-pack-a-day habit. He cocked his head at Bailey but addressed Dylan. "What'd you bring her for? We ain't on the best of terms."

"We're here to question you about the two women who recently went missing."

Edgar's face mottled, and his scowl deepened. "That ain't got nothin' to do with me. What kinda stories that bitch been telling you, eh? The truth ain't in that one."

"Let's keep this civil, Mr. Slacomb. I won't tolerate that kind of language about my partner."

"She a cop now?" Edgar spit on the ground before sparing her a malevolent glance. "Don't see no badge."

"Ranger Covington is assisting me in this matter, and you'll accord her the same respect as you do me."

Which meant nothing to Edgar, because the man had no respect for anybody. He folded his arms and regarded them sullenly.

"I understand you know the area well," Dylan continued. "Have a johnboat you use for fishing the swamp?"

"Yeah. So? I got a license. No crime there."

"Heard you like to fish along the orange water trail by Billy's Island," Dylan noted. "We found a body there yesterday."

"What? You tryin' to pin somethin' on me? Can't a man fish in peace no more?" Edgar rounded on Bailey. "What kind of nonsense you been tellin' the law 'bout me? Why, you little—"

"That's enough," Dylan cut in.

Anger overcame her initial timidity, and Bailey stepped in front of her former tormentor. "Shut. Up," she said slowly, her words measured and clipped. "For once in your miserable life, try listening and using your brain instead of antagonizing others."

Edgar flung the cigarette from his mouth and ground it into the dirt with the toe of his black boot, no doubt wishing she were beneath it instead of the cigarette stub.

"Where were you three evenings ago?" Dylan asked.

Honest surprise flickered in the man's tight face. "Where I always am. Here. Go ask Millie if ya don't believe me."

Bailey stepped away from him, clicking her tongue. As if his wife would do anything but parrot Edgar's every assertion as truth. That milksop of a woman had given up on life years ago. Maybe a better woman than Bailey could forgive and forget Millie's silent acceptance when Edgar chastised her and the other foster children...but no. In Bailey's eyes, Millie's unprotested witnessing of the acts condemned her alongside the husband she chose to stay with.

"Any other witness to that?"

"No, just me and Millie watching the TV." Curiosity won out over belligerence. "Why? What happened three nights ago? Another woman gone missing 'round here?"

"Someone tried to burn down my cabin," said Bailey.

He blinked, and then snorted. "Well, it weren't me."

"Would you mind taking a polygraph test on your whereabouts that night?" Dylan asked.

"Heck, yeah, I'd mind."

He nodded and switched tactics. "Did you ever come across Amy Holley and Mary Thornton while out fishing?"

"The missing women? Seriously, you tryin' to pin murder on me?" Edgar swallowed hard. "I may a been a bit harsh with some foster kids in the past, but that don't make me a murderer."

A bit harsh? Bailey bit her tongue to keep from interrupting Dylan's questioning.

"What makes you believe they were murdered?" he continued.

"You said you found a body. I assumed…" Edgar's voice drifted off, and for the first time, a certain vulnerability crept in.

Dylan didn't reply, just stared him down.

"C'mon, man, I ain't done nothin'." Edgar's voice switched to pathetic cajoling.

"What about Clay?" asked Bailey. "You think he's capable of committing a violent crime?"

Edgar shot her a look of pure hatred before

turning to Dylan. "No. No way. Do we need to get us a lawyer or somethin'?"

"Not if you haven't done anything wrong." Dylan's hands went to his hips, drawing attention to his sidearm. "But if you were the one outside Ranger Covington's cabin two nights ago, you best not ever go near there again. Anything happens to her or her property, you're our number one suspect."

"So that's what this is about. It ain't got nothin' to do with them missing women."

"In my experience, a man with a history of violence against women who lives in proximity to where two went missing at least warrants an interview."

"Are you done now? I told you everythin'."

Dylan nodded. "We're watching you. Have a nice day." He turned as though to leave, then swung back around. "Better start keeping your dogs under control, too."

"I ain't broke no law. There's no leash law out here in the county."

"Doesn't matter. If I believe they pose a clear threat to the community, I can send the humane officer here to round them up."

"The dog catcher?" Horror sagged Edgar's face.

Bailey knew he cared about those dogs more than any person, even his wife and brother. He'd trained them from pups to be aggressive and to "protect" him and his property.

"I'll keep 'em in the house or in the fenced backyard," Edgar grudgingly conceded. "But they wouldn't hurt a fly."

The bite marks scarring her right thigh were a testimony to that lie.

As Dylan headed to the cruiser, Bailey stood her ground until Edgar made eye contact with her.

"Liar," she said simply. "And we both know the kind of man you really are. What you're capable of doing."

She let the dead weight of her words fully settle between them, daring Edgar to deny the truth. He gaped at her, apparently at a loss as to how to respond to an adult Bailey, one who was no longer powerless and silent.

Bailey returned to the car and slammed the door shut, allowing herself one last glance at Edgar leaning against the garage, shoulders slumped, and then at the old ranch house, where Millie's pale face peeked out from behind a dingy lace curtain. Several huge dogs surrounded her, teeth bared and barking furiously. Bailey turned away and breathed more freely as the car rumbled down the dirt road and again entered the county highway.

"You okay?" Dylan asked her at last.

"I'm fine, actually." It'd been unexpectedly

satisfying to confront Edgar, to show him that she was no longer a defenseless child he could bully. She even suspected that Dylan planned the whole thing to give her an opportunity to face her demons from a position of strength. But she was nothing if not truthful. "To be honest, though, I don't think Edgar's our guy. Now, Clay, that's another story."

"Let's see what's happening on that end." Dylan punched out a number on his cell phone. "Jeff? Y'all talked to Clay yet?" Pause. "What time is he due back? Ten minutes, okay. Hold on."

Dylan lowered the phone and shot her a quizzical look. "Clay's out giving a private boat tour, but he's due back in ten minutes or so. The outfitter shop is on our way back to town. You want to talk to him, or should we let someone else?"

"I vote we interview him, too."

Might as well cut down another Goliath from her past. Seemed she was on a roll today.

Chapter Nine

He was late.

Dylan paced the loading dock, impatient to question Clay.

"He'll be here soon, don't worry," Greg Ridley, the owner of the outfitting company, assured him.

"Tour guides don't follow exact schedules," Bailey explained to Dylan. "Sometimes we'd take a little longer exploring with the guests, depending on what they were interested in seeing. I used to work here," she explained at his raised brow. "Afternoons and summers in high school, then summers in college. I loved every moment."

He imagined she'd love any job that got her away from the Slacomb residence. No wonder she loved the swamp.

"One of the best guides I ever had," Greg said, beaming at her as though she were his own daughter. "She started off working the concession stand, graduated to running the store merchandise register and then transitioned to tour guide. Kind of hate she got her forestry degree and left us, but Bailey deserved more than I could give her at this outfit."

They all stopped talking and gazed at the water trail's mouth. The sound of the approaching flat-bottomed boat could be heard before it was seen.

"Is there a problem with Clay Slacomb I should be aware of?" Greg asked. "He's well qualified and polite enough with the tourists, but I have to admit he's a loner. A bit of an odd duck. Has no interest in getting to know his coworkers. He shows up five minutes before a scheduled tour and immediately leaves once it's over. No hobnobbing with anyone."

"We're just questioning people familiar with the area," he answered evasively.

"Notice you're not questioning me or anyone else on staff this time," Greg said, tugging at his long gray beard. "If the man has anything to do with those missing women, or has some knowledge he hasn't shared, he's a real liability for my business."

Greg was an aging hippie who passionately loved nature and wildlife. He and his wife, Alma, had settled into the perfect business, an ecoadventure outfitting company, which allowed him to spend most of his time outdoors and earn a comfortable living.

The boat chugged into the shallow waters and headed for the dock. A middle-aged couple clad in T-shirts, shorts and baseball hats sipped cans of soda. A lean, scruffy man with rusty hair and a beard sat at the helm, dressed in long sleeves and long pants. Swampers knew to cover their limbs before venturing deep into the marsh. Clay had the same build as his brother—wiry and small of stature. Although one was a redhead and the other had brown hair, they both had a wary look on their faces and dark eyes that shone with suspicion and constant shifting, as though they were trapped animals pursuing an exit strategy.

He'd seen Clay from a distance over the years. The man had been brought in from time to time for public drunkenness, bar fights, disturbing the peace and, last year, a few domestic disputes. He'd never crossed the line resulting in a physical assault charge, but his girlfriend at the time had felt justifiably threatened and called for help after each incident. Thankfully, she'd decided enough was enough and split.

Had Clay sought new women to bully? And had that escalated to abduction and murder? So far, he was their best suspect.

The boat bumped against the platform and Greg started over to the dock.

"Don't mention we're here," Dylan said. "We'll wait for him near your store."

Greg nodded appreciatively. "Might not look good for business to have cops around waiting to question my employee. Thanks."

Dylan hadn't done it for Greg's benefit, but if it helped out a guy who'd befriended Bailey when she'd most needed a friend, then he was glad. As Greg hurried to the dock to lend a hand tying up the boat, Dylan motioned to Bailey, and they retreated into the shadows of the outfitter building.

The older couple exited the boat first, surprisingly spry for their age. The woman made a beeline to the restroom on the far side of the building while the man went inside the store. At the dock, Clay unloaded a cooler and then hopped aboard the platform. He scooped the heavy cooler up in one hand, and it tilted his body to the right as he made his way up the dock.

Once Clay was within six feet of them, Dylan stepped out of the shadows.

"May I have a word with you, Mr. Slacomb?"

Clay stopped dead in his tracks and regarded them warily. "Eh? What's this about? I ain't done nothin' wrong."

"We're not accusing you of a crime. We merely want to ask you a few questions—"

"Did that bitch call and file a complaint? I knew it! Flaky as heck that one."

Dylan removed a notebook from his front uniform pocket. "May I have the name of this woman?"

"You don't know?" He shook his head. "'Course you already know it. You're just messin' with me."

Paranoid little dude, Dylan decided. He'd play that card to his advantage. "Name, please. Cooperate with us and we'll get to the bottom of this."

"Nancy Mims," Clay admitted grudgingly. "We been out a few times. I swear I thought she was at least nineteen. How was I supposed to know she weren't seventeen yet? Anyways, we got in a fight and I might have pushed her away when she came at me, all jealous about another woman I was talking to. I left Nancy there at the bar. Spiteful little witch. What kind of lie she done told you?"

Shoving an underage girl? It was all the excuse he needed. Dylan shut the notepad and stuffed it back in his shirt. "Let's discuss this at the station."

His only warning was the microsecond that Clay's eyes shifted to the left. The cooler dropped out of his hand followed by an explosion of ice and soda cans rolling along the sidewalk. Clay ran, fast as a twitchy rabbit exiting a fox's lair.

Damn it. Dylan took off after him, determined to overtake Clay before he reached the tree line only twenty yards away. Bailey sped along beside him and he shook his head. No way he'd compromise her safety with a desperate man.

"Stay back and call for backup," he ordered, never breaking his stride.

"Gotcha," she called out.

The sun flashed on Clay's coppery hair, urging Dylan forward like a beacon. He had to get the guy before he disappeared into the woods. Clay reached the first copse of trees and never looked back, darting into the wilderness like a hunted animal.

Dylan plunged into the dense underbrush, felt palmetto needles slashing through his pants and flaying his legs. Not far ahead, he heard Clay's heavy footfalls as he ran. Twigs snapped, and branches whipped as he ran deeper.

"Stop," Dylan called out. His shoes sank an inch into the wet peat. Water seeped through the leather and sucked the bottom of his shoes more with each step, slowing his progress. Clay, he remembered, had been wearing knee-high wading boots. A tactical advantage—along with his intimate knowledge of this area.

Another flash of red broke through the thick shadows. Clay was at least fifty yards ahead of him now.

"Stop," he called again. "I just want to talk to you."

More frantic rustling as the suspect leaped

and skipped further into the Okefenokee. And then silence.

Blood rushed through his ears, a whir louder than the swamp's constant buzzing of insects. His chest was on fire, burning with each deep breath. He strained his ears to pick up any noise, but all he heard was his own labored breathing sawing in and out of his chest.

Stupid, stupid move on Clay's part. Did he really think he could escape a manhunt? But then, nobody had probably ever accused him of being too bright. The man was only making it harder on himself when he eventually was caught. Mentally, Dylan added fleeing a cop to the bevy of charges Clay was about to be slapped with.

He pushed forward. If the suspect was within hearing distance, perhaps he still had a chance to persuade him to give up his flight.

"Come on, Clay. Let's go to the station and talk this through man to man. What do you say? Running from me doesn't look good for you. If you're innocent like you claim, all of this can blow over. By tonight, you'll be back home."

An even more profound silence greeted his words. "Damn it, Slacomb. Quit this foolishness."

Twigs snapped somewhere close to his right and he spun around, drawing his gun. "That you, Slacomb? Come out with your hands up."

Odds were that Clay had no weapon, but he

wasn't taking chances. More rustling ensued, and Dylan held his gun steady, aimed and ready to fire. From the thicket, a doe emerged, terrified and snorting a warning. She thundered past him and disappeared again into the woods, her hooves pounding the peat. He slowly holstered his weapon, wondering which of them had suffered the greater scare at the unexpected encounter.

He was at a distinct disadvantage here. Clay knew this swamp better than him.

"WHICH WAY DO you think Clay's heading?" Bailey asked Greg as she hung up her cell phone. "If he keeps straight he's headed to the Lily Pad prairie."

Greg hustled up beside her, panting. "I can't believe he ran."

"Which direction do you think he's going?" she asked again.

"He might take the green trail and head on home. His place is only three miles in that direction, off of Blankenship Road."

She thought fast. "I can cut him off at the mouth of the trail. He's gotta cross it to get back home."

"Shouldn't we wait on the cops to chase him down?"

"That'll take too long. Just give me the keys to your fastest boat."

Greg shook his head and turned to run back to the dock. "I'm going with you. Hurry."

Alma, Greg's wife, hurried out of the building and caught up to them as they ran across the pier. "Greg? What's going on? Something wrong?"

Quickly, Bailey began untying the rope as Greg jumped in the boat.

"It's okay," he assured Alma. "Cops will be arriving shortly. Tell them Bailey and I are headed to the egret prairie."

"But—"

Greg started the motor, cutting off Alma's protest, and Bailey hopped on board. Greg revved the engine and they sped out of the small marina, for once careless of the wake breaking over the old platform dock boards. Her former boss pushed the small boat to its maximum speed and they busted through the narrow Tater Rake Run Trail heavily lined with hoorah bushes and ty ty shrubs, then navigated between islands thick with maidencane and rose pogonia.

Lazy alligators slowly slithered from the banks as they espied the racing boat. They were more frightened of humans than vice versa.

The first water prairie they sludged through was populated with batteries of floating peat abloom with pitcher plants, and the copper reeds of broomsedge. Bailey kept her eyes peeled along the banks, hoping for signs of human movement, but nothing appeared out of the ordinary. Greg channeled them through another short, narrow water trail and then abruptly shut off the boat engine.

"If he was headin' home, Clay can't run further than this point. Water's too deep and too wide. But could be he has a small boat or canoe cached 'round here. A few days last month he came to work by boat because his car was broken."

They both fixed their gaze on the shoreline, eyes and ears straining for signs of life as Greg slowly navigated the boat parallel to the bank.

"Can't believe Clay would hunt down those women," Greg said at last. "But running off like he did sure makes him look guilty."

"I wouldn't put anything past the man," she answered sharply.

"Just because Clay is Edgar's brother doesn't mean he's cut from the same cloth."

She kept her lips fused into a tight line, refusing to give voice to the memories. Did Clay even remember her? Or was she some throwaway kid that he'd seen mistreated and then immediately wiped from his consciousness? She picked up the binoculars Greg always kept in the seat compartment and trained them on the shore. Minutes later, she discerned the faint outline of an old, dented johnboat leaning against a cypress tree.

"Bingo," she said, pointing to the tree. "Found his boat. Let's land here."

They pulled up to the bank, their boat landing with a soft thud. Greg handed her the rope they used to tie up the boat, picked up an oar he kept stored for potential motor malfunctions and gripped it tightly. "In case I need a weapon," he told her. "But I have a good relationship with Clay. Shouldn't be necessary to use force to subdue him if he comes our way."

"You know what we could do?" she said, thinking aloud. "If we take Clay's boat, then we might not need to fight him at all. He'll see he can't escape and he'll give himself up."

"Always knew you were a smart girl," Greg said with a chuckle.

She shrugged dismissively. "You'd have thought of it, too, eventually."

But his praise warmed her. Her former boss had a master's degree in biology and knew the species of every plant in the swamp as well as the behavior patterns of every bird, reptile and wildlife animal that called this lonely place home. His wisdom and kindness had inspired her life's path as a forest ranger.

Together, they hauled Clay's boat from the bank. Greg waded further into the water and began tying Clay's boat to their skiff.

Out of nowhere, a loud rustling filled the air

and she went still, unsure if it was a deer or a man. Crashing footfalls blasted from the wood's dark interior and then Clay stumbled forward. His eyes were wild and hunted as he blinked, assessing this new danger.

"Give it up, Clay," Greg called out, the rope still in his hands where he was yoking the two boats together.

Clay bent over double, one hand clutching his stomach, the other anchored on a knee. His panting was loud and labored. From behind, Dylan crashed through the woods. Clay's posture slumped a bit further, as though conceding defeat at being covered front and back. Still, his eyes focused on her and, oddly, seemed to burn into hers. It'd been so long ago that he'd dismissed his brother's treatment of her with nothing but a smirk. But did he recognize her now?

His head raised, and he grunted an acknowledgment. "I remember you. Bonnie? Brenda? Always were trouble."

Bailey gave a quick tap to the crow feather nestled at her breastbone. Lulu's custom talisman always provided the needed boost of strength for any situation.

Without warning, Clay pulled a slapjack from his pants pocket. She'd seen that weapon once before when Edgar and Clay had had a drunken fight one evening. The black leather baton was about eight inches in length and filled with buck-shot. Her eyes fixated on the slapjack and her vision tunneled. A splash sounded behind her; Greg had slipped and fallen into the water.

Clay charged forward. A mad bull, intent on his target.

Her mind swiftly calculated the odds of help. Greg still splashed in the water, evidently trying to regain his footing. Dylan shouted something, but she couldn't say what, only that he'd never get to her in time to prevent an attack.

She was on her own.

Clay might hurt her, but she wasn't going down without getting in a few licks of her own.

She'd show him that she was no longer a silent, passive victim.

She'd fight for that lost girl who'd taken so much at the hands of her foster father.

And she'd prove to herself that no man could mistreat her and not suffer a consequence.

The air around her stirred with Clay's charge. Instead of running away, Bailey swiftly bent forward and moved sideways, ramming his rib cage. A satisfying grunt of pain escaped his lips before he grabbed her arm and they both fell to the ground. The impact knocked loose his bruising grip. Quickly she rolled over, scrambling to her feet.

Clay was a second ahead of her. He loomed above, blocking the sun, the slapjack held high in his right hand. With a *whoosh*, it descended. Bailey lunged to the right, trying to escape its inevitable impact, but its leaded weight crashed against her left shoulder. Fire welted along her flesh and her eyes went teary from pain. Her traitorous knees turned to jelly, and she crumbled. Another whir from above and she knew what was coming. Before the blow landed, Bailey grabbed Clay's right calf and pulled with all her might, praying to knock him off balance.

The second strike landed on her right hip and a kaleidoscope of color burst behind her eyes, blinding her. But she felt the vibration of the wet peat as Clay landed beside her, cursing. She kicked at him as two male voices barked at one another from somewhere above. Help had at last arrived.

She blinked through the pain and watched as Greg struggled to hold Clay's kicking feet while Dylan grappled with Clay's arms and shoulders. Together, the two managed to roll Clay onto his belly. Dylan slapped on handcuffs, the metal clicking loud and reassuring her of her safety. Greg, ever resourceful, tied Clay's feet together with his boat rope.

Once the cuffs were secured, Dylan darted her a wild glance. "How bad are you hurt, Bailey? Any broken bones?"

She slowly sat up and shook her head to clear

out the ringing. "Don't…" She inhaled sharply at the stinging pain in her shoulder and hip. "…don't think so."

Greg's arm wrapped around her. "Think you can stand? If not, I'll carry you to the boat."

No. She wouldn't give Clay the satisfaction of seeing her incapacitated. "I've got this," she protested. "Just lend me a hand."

Gritting her teeth, she stood and glared down at Clay, who writhed and cursed, even trussed like a chicken for Sunday dinner.

Dylan gave her a somber nod before he returned his attention to the suspect. "You're under arrest," he began.

Her lips grimly curled at the corners. Squaring off with two Slacombs in one day was tough on a woman, but she'd survived. She dropped to one knee beside the still-squirming Clay and whispered in his ear, "Who's laughing now?"

Chapter Ten

"I'm okay," Bailey kept insisting to Dylan, Evan, Sheriff Chesser and the mélange of cops and federal agents when they'd returned to the sheriff station. "Really. It was only a couple of hits from a slapjack. I don't need to go home and take it easy."

But they insisted, and she reluctantly gave in after Dylan promised to drop by her cabin in the evening to update her on the investigation. Driving home, she felt the pain in her shoulder and hip deepen, and she gripped the steering wheel to steady her body's sudden tremors. She hadn't counted on this delayed onslaught of nerves. Her teeth chattered, and as though her car was on autopilot, she was driving down her road with no clear memory of navigating.

Her mind played another trick on her as, without a conscious plan of action, she sped past her own cabin and pulled into Lulu's dirt driveway. The blue pickup parked by the side of Lulu's place took her by surprise. Holt was back in town. She threw her car in Reverse to leave, not wanting to interrupt their time together.

The front door banged open and Lulu emerged onto the porch, beckoning her to come inside. Bailey stuck her head out the window and waved. "That's okay. Didn't know you had company. I'll see ya later."

"Don't you dare run off." Lulu hurried toward the car, her face drawn with concern. "Heard 'bout what happened with that Slacomb boy. How bad you hurt?"

Should have known this morning's events would have spread all over town. "I'm fine," she answered, for what seemed like the hundredth time today.

"I got just the thing for you. Come on in."

"But Holt's here—"

"So what?"

"I don't want to intrude."

Lulu scowled and pivoted toward the porch, expecting Bailey to follow.

She did. Not because she felt up to a social call, but because if she didn't visit, Lulu would merely show up at her cabin and demand entrance. Might as well get this over with. After all, it was her own fault for coming over in the first place.

Inside, Holt stood and strode over, his weath-

ered face echoing Lulu's concern. He held out a
hand and she shook it. "How bad did that man
hurt you, darlin'?"

"I'm fine." She repeated the words by rote.

Lulu pointed at the couch and Bailey sat, almost sighing at the relief of taking the weight off
her shaky legs. Holt brought her a glass of iced
tea and she swallowed a long draft. Lulu hovered
over the couch, holding a small tin container.

"Where'd he strike you? This'll take the sting
right out," she promised, scooping a bit of yellow salve on her index finger.

The room filled with the cooling scent of peppermint and some earthy smell Bailey couldn't
identify. "I can put it on at home," she said.

"Where?" Lulu asked, ignoring her protest.

Bailey sighed and pushed aside a couple of
inches of her uniform blouse. "Left shoulder and
neck."

She closed her eyes and tried not to wince at
Lulu's touch. The salve stung for a second, and
then the cooling began to numb the sting.

"What's in this magic elixir?"

"A large dose of peppermint mixed with cas-
tor oil and beeswax from my own hives. I also
put in Saint-John's-wort and Solomon's seal for
speedy healing."

"It's awesome. Thanks."

"Anywhere else you need it?"

Bailey cast a significant nod at Holt. "I'll, um, take care of that at home."

"I'll leave the room," he quickly volunteered, making a move toward the hall.

"No, don't. I'm going home." Lulu's mouth opened to protest, but Bailey spoke quickly. "I just want to lie down and rest," she lied. Her friend couldn't argue with that sentiment.

"Humph." Lulu gave her a squinty I-don't-trust-you side-glance. "At least let me take care of your talisman. Hand me your necklace."

Bailey pulled the leather cord over her neck and placed it in Lulu's palm, already knowing the brief ceremony her friend wanted to perform. This was at least the third time she'd had to cleanse the bad juju and replace the crow feather. Feathers didn't hold up well against sweaty skin during the humid Georgia summers.

Lulu retrieved a new crow feather from her desk drawer, then lit a sage smudge stick. The acrid-sweet smoke wisped around the new plume while Lulu mumbled a quick prayer.

"I'll bury the old one," Holt offered. Although only one-sixteenth Native American, he was well versed in their customs and held the old ways in respect. He unhooked it from the leather cord and exited the back door.

Finished with the blessing, Lulu took the necklace to the sink and rinsed water over the turquoise beads and obsidian to purify them. "That should do it," she pronounced, returning the talisman to Bailey.

The stones lay heavy and smooth in her hand, the new feather tickling her palm. Bailey wasn't convinced that the ritual was necessary, but she couldn't deny that the necklace provided her comfort and strength. The talisman helped, and she wasn't messing with what worked.

"Thank you," she murmured. "I'll be on my way. Tell Holt thanks, too. When did he get back in town?"

"Got back this morning from an expedition in Maggie Valley, North Carolina. Says he doesn't have another one booked for nearly a month."

"Good." Lulu would never admit it, but Bailey guessed her existence was often a lonely one. She enjoyed working with her beehives and gardening but had little interaction with people.

Driving home, niggling worries scrabbled through her mind. She wasn't lonely like Lulu, was she? After all, she had her job and coworkers.

What about friends? What about family? What about a lover?

Not her fault she had no family—and Lulu was her best friend. Okay, her only friend. Everybody else was merely an acquaintance.

And a lover? Dylan's face sprang into her consciousness, a handsome picture with kind, olive green eyes and sandy hair that curled slightly at the ends. Maybe. She couldn't deny she was attracted to him, even if he was an Armstrong. With an effort, she shrugged off the thought. Getting attacked and confronting two enemies in one day had rattled her, that's all.

All she wanted to do was take a couple of ibuprofen, get a bath and then apply Lulu's salve on her injuries. But when she got home, she groaned at the sight of the park management vehicle in her driveway.

Evan exited his car and watched as she parked her vehicle and then approached. She lifted her chin and painted on a breezy smile. "Hi, Evan. What brings you here?"

"Came to check on you."

"I'm fine," she said once again.

"It's just the two of us now."

The intensity in his eyes made her uncomfortable, especially when he stepped in a little closer.

"You can tell me if you're hurting."

She opened her mouth to deny it, then snapped it shut. Once she told Evan what he wanted to hear, he'd leave. "Okay, it stings a little. But it's not like I've got broken bones or anything."

"You're always so brave." Evan laid a hand on her shoulder. The weight on her tender flesh sent pain shooting through her arm. She hissed in pain.

"Sorry, I forgot that's where you're hurt."

Evan closed the distance between them, pulled her to his chest and patted her between her shoulder blades.

Surely he wasn't putting a move on her—was he? It must be her imagination.

"If you don't mind, I'm going inside now to rest. Been a crazy day."

"Poor Bailey." He pulled back and looked at her with an intense gleam in his eyes. "Let me take care of you."

"I don't need taking care of," she replied tartly. "See you tomorrow morning, Evan."

With that, she spun on her heels and stepped away, determined to shake off the unwanted advance.

"Wait." His hand grabbed her elbow.

"That's enough, Evan. I'm going inside. Alone."

"But I only want to—"

"The lady said *that's enough*," a male voice boomed.

She swore she'd never seen a more welcome sight than Dylan's stern face as he stared down her boss.

Evan let her go and raised his hands, palms up. An aw-shucks expression crossed his face. "It's not what you think. I only came by to see how Bailey's doing." He turned to her, his eyes oddly pleading. "Isn't that right, Bailey?"

Confusion knotted her brow. Maybe she'd read something into their exchange that wasn't there. They'd worked together for years without so much as an inappropriate comment passing his lips. For her part, she'd regarded him as something of a father figure. Not that she'd ever had a role model for how a normal father-daughter relationship really worked. Her biological father had never been in the picture and Edgar Slacomb had surely demonstrated the worst possible example of fatherhood.

She was spared answering Evan when Dylan spoke up. "You've expressed your concern and seen that she's fine. Best be on your way, then, Mr. Johnson," he said coolly.

"Yes, yes, of course." Evan shuffled toward his car and waved casually. "Glad you're okay, Bailey."

The speed with which he started his car and backed out of her driveway was almost comical. She'd have laughed if she didn't dread the inevitable awkwardness of their next encounter.

Dylan stood beside her, watching Evan as he drove out of sight. "I don't like that man," he said slowly.

"Evan's okay. I'm sure that—whatever *that* was—won't happen again."

"It better not."

"If it does, I'll put him quickly in his place."

"Promise?"

"Absolutely."

He nodded. "Are you really okay? It's been one heck of a day for you so far."

"If one more person asks me that…"

Dylan laughed as he walked to his car. "Got someone here who wants to say hello."

He bent inside the vehicle and emerged holding twenty pounds of squirming, tail-wagging canine.

"Ace!" She laughed, surprised at the burst of warmth that exploded in her chest as the dog yipped a happy reply. Then she spotted the bandage on his haunch. "Is he doing okay?"

"Vet says he is. Like you, I expect Ace is sick of people mooning over his injury. He wants out and about."

He set the dog on the ground and Ace scurried over, limping only slightly. Tentatively, she bent down and patted the top of his head.

"Now there's progress for you," Dylan said, his voice smug with satisfaction.

She looked up at him. "Doesn't mean I want him slobbering all over me."

"Of course." Dylan whistled, and Ace reluctantly hobbled to his side and sat, regarding her with a wistful cock of his head as his tail thumped the ground.

"It's blazing hot out here. Want to come inside?" she asked impulsively. Never mind that a minute ago she'd wanted nothing more than to be alone. Dylan seemed to have a positive, calming effect on her mood.

"Thought you'd never ask. Want me to leash Ace on your porch railing?"

Ace emitted a tiny high-pitched whimper, as though he understood their conversation and needed to voice his desire to stay with them. How could she refuse?

"He can come in, too. As long as he behaves."

They followed her onto the porch and she unlocked the door.

"You smell like—" he took a deep sniff "—Christmas candy," Dylan observed.

She laughed. "Lulu's special concoction for pain. It really does seem to take some of the sting out."

"Ah, right. Your friend down the road."

They entered the cabin and she led them to the kitchen, where she set Lulu's elixir on the table and then filled a bowl of water for Ace.

"Are you thirsty?"

"I wouldn't turn down a glass of water. Thanks."

She grabbed two water bottles from the fridge and they sat at the table side by side. "What's happening with Clay Slacomb?"

"For now, he's being held for assaulting an officer."

"How long can you keep him locked up on that charge?"

"A few days at least. Long enough to give us time to dig a little more and see if any forensic evidence shows up to pin him to these crimes."

She picked at the plastic wrapping on her bottle. "I can't stop thinking about Amy Holley. Wondering if she's still alive. If she's in pain. She must be so scared."

"We'll find her, or…" He abruptly closed his mouth.

"Or she might meet the same fate as her sister?" Bailey supplied.

"We don't know for sure that her sister is dead. There's a large force out searching the entire Okefenokee. They've even got the heat-seeking helicopter coming in the morning. Everything that can be done is being done."

She nodded and gazed out the window at the thick copse of trees that stretched as far as the eye could see. The swamp was vast and there were most likely areas of it that no one had ever roamed. A man—or woman—could easily get lost and stay lost in that vastness.

Ace, curled up on her kitchen rug, snored noisily, snapping her back to the present moment.

Bailey squared her shoulders. "What's our next step? Where do we go from here?"

"You tell me. So far, your hunches have been spot-on. Without you, we'd still be nowhere in this investigation."

She bit her lip, desperately trying to decide what search location might prove fruitful. "All that comes to mind at the moment is Chesser Island, although I have to admit it's a stretch. Too public. Our guy would be extremely brazen to use the Chesser homestead to hold his victim. We do tours through it at least twice a week. Not to mention that the island now has a well-traveled road built to it. Tourists drive out there all the time on the way to the wildlife boardwalk and observation tower."

"I don't remember there being any mounds on that property, though, so it's not like the other sites we searched."

"True. But there's an old corncob shed and a defunct turpentine still at the back of the property. In their own way, you could argue that they're shrines to a way of life that no longer exists, an homage to early settlers of the swamp."

"We have nothing to lose by trying," Dylan pointed out.

"Should we go now?" Bailey glanced at the clock on the kitchen wall and half rose from her chair. "Still plenty of daylight left if we hurry."

"Heck, no."

Dylan laid a hand on her arm and her skin tingled once again—this time with warmth. Nothing like the creepy feel of Evan's touch.

Dylan's fingers traveled down her arm until he found her hand and clasped it within his own. "We've both been through the wringer today. And we both know that wherever Amy is, we won't find her curled up in bed at the Chesser homestead. If she was there, she'd have been found by now."

She couldn't argue with his logic.

"Best thing we can do is chill out, get a good night's rest this evening and then meet at dawn to start searching again."

He picked up the tin of salve and experimentally sniffed. "Yep. Makes me think of candy canes hanging on a Christmas tree."

"You should smell some of her other herbal concoctions." Bailey chuckled. "Nothing pleasant about them at all. Especially the tinctures she wants you to drink."

Dylan scooped a dollop and then brushed her hair back. "I see where he struck you."

He lightly applied more of the cooling salve and it helped numb the welt's heat, although it did set off a warmth in her core that had nothing to do with this morning's attack and everything to do with Dylan. He undid the first button of her shirt and the feel of his hands so near her breasts set her heart pounding. He lifted her necklace, observing her collection of talismans before slanting her a hooded glance. "Beautiful," he murmured.

Bailey wasn't sure if he was referring to her or the necklace, so she didn't respond.

His fingers slid down the rest of the welt, and then he ever-so-slowly rebuttoned her shirt.

"Thanks," she croaked.

His voice was equally as gruff. "I read the incident report. He also struck you on the hip."

"Yes, well. Never mind that. I'll take care of it myself."

"Why don't you let me help you?" He breathed the question into her ear, sending a shiver of passion that shot straight to her core and made her thighs tightly squeeze together. It was obvious he wanted more than to merely soothe the throbbing welt inflicted by the slapjack.

Why not? At the moment, she couldn't muster a single objection. It'd been a heck of a day, so why shouldn't she give in to her desire? He wanted her, too; she could tell by the smolder in his eyes and the palpable charge that now arced between them. Initially she'd resented him because of who his father was and how he'd betrayed her. But she'd put the past behind her.

She'd proven it today by facing the Slacomb brothers and emerging relatively unscathed.

That initial tension had morphed into an awareness, then an attraction. An attraction that she could no longer deny.

Bailey stood, picked up the salve and took Dylan's hand. He scrabbled to his feet, olive eyes darkening and glowing, fierce with need. She led him down the hallway and into her small bedroom, their hands still joined. She released his hand and slowly slipped out of her shirt and shorts, her skin tingling as he watched her with hawkish concentration. Easing onto the bed, she held out the tin to Dylan.

He sat beside her, and his hands trembled slightly as he unscrewed the top. That slight hint of his nervousness eradicated her own. Whatever was between them, Dylan did not take it lightly, and she found the knowledge reassuring. Bailey lay on her side and drew down the edge of her lace panties, exposing the welt on her hip. With bated breath, she awaited his touch.

His fingers slid along the curve of her hip, and she marveled at the gentleness of his touch as he skimmed her injury with the salve. The stinging numbed instantly, and she promptly forgot all about it, consumed only with the fire that roared to life at his touch.

The edge of her panties eased down her sensitive skin as he finished applying the salve. Then he carefully replaced her panties over the injury. She closed her eyes and anticipated what she hoped was coming next.

Instead of his whispered murmurs of seduction, all she heard was the thump of the tin can on her nightstand and the gasp that burst through his lips.

"What the heck?" he asked loudly, breaking the seductive mood.

Alarmed, she rolled over and faced him. "What's wrong?"

His hand found the inside of her right thigh, and his fingers grazed the scars that ran in half-moon circles from midthigh to her knees.

"Childhood accident," she muttered, pushing his hand away. "Forget about it."

"Accident, heck. Those are bite marks."

"And now you know why dogs freak me out," she said, striving for a light, casual tone. "I was attacked once."

His face looked incredulous, outrage shining in his eyes and a hard set to his jaw. "By what? A pack of wild pit bulls?"

"Dobermans, actually. Can you just let it go? I don't want to talk about that right now."

Understanding gleamed in his eyes. "Edgar Slacomb's Dobermans?"

"Yes."

"How did it happen?"

She bit her lip and shrugged, as though the old injury was of no consequence. "Doesn't matter."

"The heck it doesn't." He wrapped her right hand in both of his own and squeezed—an offering of sympathy and reassurance. "I want to know," he urged softly. "I want to know everything about you."

No one had ever said that to her before. Other men had noticed her scars while in bed and had offered a fleeting sympathy before moving on to have sex, but none had taken the time to question her further.

Her eyes teared up—not from a painful memory, but from Dylan's caring.

"I was sixteen," she said. "Fed up with my foster family and desperate to escape. So one night when I'd had enough, I snuck out of the house with an overnight bag stuffed with everything I owned in the world." She sat up in bed, tucking a pillow behind her as she leaned against the headboard.

"I'd squirreled away a bit of cash from working at Greg's place, whatever Edgar didn't manage to steal from my paycheck, and I knew the lay of the land. I thought it'd be enough to get away, but…" She hesitated, remembering what it'd felt like to flee in the darkness. A mixture of fear and excitement as adrenaline had flooded every cell of her body and freedom seemed within her grasp. She'd imagined herself invincible. Strong, smart and daring.

But Edgar had been older and more clever.

The dogs circled the edge of his property at night, and although she'd waited until they were asleep, they'd roused at her quiet movement as she'd fled to the woods. Even now, the memory of their feverish barking set her heart pumping in overdrive.

"Edgar's dogs chased you down," Dylan said flatly. His eyes squeezed shut as he took in her story.

The dogs had circled her, snapping their jaws and baring their fangs. A few lunged from time to time, nipping and tearing her jeans. But their aggression had been contained until Edgar arrived on the scene, his face a mask of fury. He'd sent away the pack, save the alpha. *Sic her*, Edgar had screamed.

"Even after being cornered, I didn't believe they'd hurt me. Edgar had them well trained to only attack on command."

"But they did, anyway."

"After being ordered to—yes."

"Edgar ordered them to attack you?" Dylan asked slowly, his words weighted with anger.

"Only one of them. If the whole pack had attacked, I don't think I'd have lived through it."

Dylan didn't speak for several heartbeats, then stood and paced the room, his body taut with outrage. "Unbelievable. I'll make Slacomb pay for that. I promise you, Bailey."

"It's over," she said quietly. "It hurt, but I survived. Can we drop this now, please?"

Indecision warred on his face. He clearly didn't want to let the matter drop, but he didn't want to upset her any more, either.

"For now," he agreed, returning to sit on her bed. He cupped her face in his hands. "I'm sorry this happened to you."

"Thanks, but I don't want your pity. It was a long time ago. Can we just concentrate on us now?" she asked.

He shook his head, as though to clear it of the horror of what she'd shared.

"Just so you know, I think you're an amazing woman. Strong, courageous and resourceful. You survived trauma and refused to let it stop you from pursuing a challenging career and then working with me to catch a killer."

It was probably the nicest compliment she'd ever received. She blinked back tears at the warm words and the tender glow in his eyes. Instead of viewing her fear of dogs as a sign of weakness, he chose to focus on her determination to help other victims.

"Thank you," she breathed. She hated anyone

seeing this vulnerable side of her, but Dylan had made her feel safe and hadn't belittled her fear. Her estimation of his character grew. He was not his father. He was his own man. One she wanted to know intimately.

Bailey tilted her chin up and whispered, "You're a little overdressed for what I have in mind." Her hands began to unbutton the front of his uniform shirt. At his sharp intake of breath, a smile curled her lips.

Evidently she wasn't moving fast enough for Dylan, and he quickly finished unbuttoning the rest of his shirt. "Are you sure about this?" he asked, his voice gruff.

"I've never been more sure."

In one fell swoop, he pulled the shirt off.

Bailey ran her fingers through the curly hair on his chest and then frowned at the bruise a mere three inches above his heart. Clay Slacomb's knuckles had left an imprint from this morning's tussle.

"You're hurt, too."

"It's minor."

His lips pressed against hers, tender and exploratory at first, and then deepening with passion. All thoughts of the Slacombs and their brutality were cleansed by the searing heat of desire. Her pulse quickened and heat spread through her like fever. The scent of his amber aftershave intoxicated her further.

Dylan drew her into his arms, and she laid her head against his chest, feeling the strong, steady hammer of his heart against the side of her face. She traced the fingers of her right hand down the sinewy muscle of his left arm and when she reached his calloused palm, he clasped her small hand in his and squeezed, offering reassurance.

His hands then roamed her back, exploring and leaving behind a trail of fire wherever he touched her. She ached for him to be inside her, and her hands did their own exploring. His body was splendid—strong, hard and smooth. A perfect complement to her soft curves.

With no embarrassment, she rose and pulled off all her clothes. His eyes glowed appreciatively as she stood naked before him. Quickly, he shed the rest of his clothes. He held out his hand to her and she took it, allowing him to draw her close, bare skin to bare skin.

And as he claimed her, she responded with everything she had—mind, body and soul aligned with Dylan. If only she could contain this magic, store it up and tuck it away like a treasure to be relived forever—because she'd never experienced anything like it before and doubted she ever would again once this case was over and they returned to their separate lives.

Chapter Eleven

Dylan fought hard not to keep stealing glances at Bailey next to him in the vehicle. Memories of last night's lovemaking kept flitting through his mind—the sound and feel and smell and taste of her. He wished they could have stayed in bed forever.

He tried to squash a grin as he remembered that sometime during the night while they slumbered, Ace had crawled to the foot of the bed and gone to sleep. At a particularly loud doggy snore, Bailey had startled awake and glared at the pooch. But she hadn't kicked Ace to the curb, and Dylan viewed it as a real sign of progress.

His amusement faded as he remembered why Bailey feared dogs. Someday, somehow, Edgar Slacomb would pay for his cruelty to Bailey. He'd never, ever allow anyone to mistreat her again.

The worst of the late-afternoon heat had passed. In spite of their plans to search the island at first light, they'd been called into Chesser's office to be updated on the latest developments and to map out a new plan of action.

Evan had acted overly polite and stiff at the meeting, evidently realizing he'd overstepped his bounds yesterday. As much as possible, he'd avoided speaking directly to either of them—and that suited Dylan just fine.

He and Bailey had submitted their proposal to search the Chesser homestead and then spend the night there if they found any promising leads. It was a long shot, but they hoped the killer might return to his crime scene or to check on a buried trophy. Evan's eyes had twitched at the mention of them sharing an all-night stakeout, but he'd clamped his jaw shut and offered no objection. Sheriff Chesser had agreed to their plan, cautioning that they were to inform him immediately if they found any leads.

"They haven't been able to crack Clay at all yet," Bailey said with a sigh, breaking into Dylan's thoughts as he drove. "If he is guilty, do you think he'll ever confess?"

"They usually sing at some point to cut a deal with the prosecution. Or, better yet, Clay might boast about his crimes to a cell mate who'll turn snitch to cut his own deal."

"What's your gut telling you about Clay?" she asked. "Do you think he has anything to do with the missing kayakers or Lisa Shaw?"

"I have my doubts. What about you?"

She let out a dispirited sigh. "I thought he was guilty at first, but now I'm not so sure."

"All we can do is keep searching the swamp while Clay's being interrogated." He tried to renew her hope. "A break will come in the case soon enough."

He pulled his car into a copse of trees twenty yards past the parking lot and made sure it was well hidden from view. They unloaded their metal detectors before walking the short distance through a well-worn trail to reach the Chesser homestead. Dylan carried Ace in the crook of his free arm, not wanting to unnecessarily tire him in the search. His boss had suggested using a different dog for the day, but Dylan had declined. Bailey wouldn't be comfortable with another canine.

Soon they reached the clearing, and he set Ace on the ground.

The place didn't have an island vibe at all. At nearly six hundred acres, the land had been joined to a paved park road and was easily accessible to the public. The last tour of the day was in progress as they reached the neat, raked property—so groomed by the early settlers to easily spot venomous snakes.

"…settled in 1858," they heard the guide explain. "The rugged Chessers hunted and trapped game and grew what they could in the sandy soil. Twice a year they went to town for salt, sugar, flour and gunpowder."

"Bor*ing*," one of the teenage tourists sang out. He turned to his parents and rolled his eyes. "I'd hate to be stuck here in the boonies like they were."

Privately, Dylan agreed with the teenager. Not much to do back then except work and suffer the heat and lack of indoor plumbing.

The guide spotted them and waved a hand, strolling over from the porch. "Mr. Johnson called ahead to say you were coming. I was just finishing up."

"No hurry," Bailey assured her. She patted the front pocket of her shorts. "I've got the key to lock up if you want to go ahead and leave."

They watched as the tourists, and a minute later the guide, exited the homestead and drove away. Ace began experimentally sniffing the ground.

"Want to search the property first?" he suggested.

"I'll take the corncob shed while you take the turpentine still."

They split paths and Dylan set to work, arcing the detector over the old wooden structure. It was slow, tedious work and he knew the odds were low they'd find any relic here. At least it gave him another opportunity to work with Bailey, and he looked forward to spending the night here with her—primitive and uncomfortable as it might prove.

And to think she'd rubbed him the wrong way in the beginning. Instead of proving an unwelcome hindrance that had been foisted upon him, Bailey had provided the crucial break in this case. It certainly hadn't been him or anyone in the sheriff's office.

In the privacy of the old still, Dylan felt his face and neck burn in humiliation. In the future, he'd be more open to input from others outside of an official investigation. Lesson learned.

Methodically, he covered every inch of ground. Distilling turpentine from pine tree bark had been a dangerous, messy business. He couldn't imagine how they'd endured the steam from the boiling water on top of the hot, humid climate.

"Dylan! Come quick!"

Was Bailey hurt or in danger? He flung the detector to the ground and ran next door to the shed.

The interior smelled pungent and he squinted his eyes at the sudden darkness. Ace barked and ran in circles around Bailey. Wordlessly, she held out her gloved hand. A gold charm nestled in her palm, and he donned his own gloves before picking up the piece and examining it.

The claddagh. Two hands, representing friend-ship, clasped a heart, symbolizing love, which was surmounted by a crown, a sign of loyalty.

"Mary Thornton has a claddagh," Bailey said tightly. "Has to be hers."

Rather, Mary *had* one—past tense. Bailey looked up from the charm, her eyes wide and full of pain. Without him saying a word, she knew what this meant as well.

Mary was most likely dead.

He took the claddagh from her hand, bagged it and glanced around the coffin-like interior of the shed. "Where did you find it?"

"Far right corner, buried only an inch under the sand." She showed him her cell phone. "I took a picture before I picked it up."

"Her body might be buried nearby, just like the other body wasn't far from the ring. I'll no-tify the sheriff."

"Wait." Her hand stayed his arm when he reached for his two-way radio. "Let's think about this a minute."

He raised a brow. "Why? We need to get the cadaver dogs out here."

"But if we don't tell anyone, we have a chance to find the killer tonight. If you call Chesser they'll set out floodlights and have dogs and search personnel crawling over every inch of this place. The killer will never return."

"We could still stake out the homestead another night. He might return for his trophy."

"No, it'd be too risky for him. News of Mary's recovered body will be all over the news by morning."

"The likelihood of him returning tonight is slim," he argued.

"But it's our best chance. Our only chance. It's tonight or never."

The idea was tempting. He wanted nothing more than to catch the killer in an act that any jury would buy as evidence of his guilt. But protocol was protocol. "Let me present that argument to my boss."

"No." She shook her head emphatically. "He'll never go along with the plan and you know it. We can say we found the claddagh the next morning. Chesser will be none the wiser."

He'd never lied to his boss before and the idea didn't sit well with him. Still, the possibility of catching the killer, no matter how remote, was too tempting to pass up.

Bailey seemed to sense him relenting. "Please. Our best hope of finding Amy alive is to find her abductor straightaway. Her time might be running out, if it hasn't already."

He drew a deep breath and took the plunge. "Where's the rake? If we don't want the killer to know we're here, we'll need to cover our tracks, especially Ace's paw prints."

"Thank you," she breathed. "The rake's on the back porch. I'll run and get it."

Ace trotted out behind Bailey and he stood alone, arms folded. Prickles of unease stabbed his gut. This hiding space was so brazen. Their killer thought himself more clever than the law enforcement officers searching for clues. What if… Dylan sucked in his breath. What if the killer was so bold because he *was* one of the cops?

Bailey returned with the rake, and he spun around as she entered the shed. His disturbing thoughts must have shown on his face.

"What is it?" she asked. "Having a change of heart?"

"No, just speculating if the killer is one of us—a police officer, that is."

"I've wondered the same thing. All the more reason to keep this discovery to ourselves until morning."

"Evan Johnson always seems to be around," he noted, thinking aloud.

Bailey blinked and then shook her head. "No way. I'd suspect *your* boss before I would mine."

"Chesser?" he said in surprise. "Never. I've known him all my life. He and my dad were good friends. The guy's straight-up decent. On the other hand, Evan pulled a creepy move yesterday hitting on you."

"It was out of character for him," she argued. "The only time he's ever stepped over a line. Maybe I misread his intentions."

"Get real. You don't really believe that, do you? Let's put his advance to the side for the moment and look at the facts. He could well be the killer. Johnson has an intimate knowledge of this swamp and access to everything in the park."

"By your logic, Sheriff Chesser looks just as guilty. He has the same familiarity of the swamp and freedom to access anything within the park. Plus, this homestead is special to him—it belonged to his family. Speaking of which, the Chesser patriarch only ran to the Okefenokee and settled here to evade a murder charge."

"He was innocent, and you know it. It was merely a fight that turned tragic. Years later, a witness came forward and defended him."

Bailey sighed. "I don't want to argue. On the off chance it's either of our bosses, that's even more reason not to report our finding tonight. Agreed?"

He weighed the pros and cons before tersely nodding his head. "Agreed."

"Good. Go on outside with Ace and I'll sweep over our footprints in the sand."

"I'll give the house a preliminary look through."

Dylan retrieved his metal detector from the still and made his way to the porch. He whistled for Ace, and the dog reluctantly left Bailey's side.

"Traitor," he mumbled under his breath. The beagle had taken a shine to his newest partner.

Dylan figured he might as well take a quick scan around the homestead's perimeter before starting inside. But neither Ace, nor the metal detector, nor his own eyes picked up anything unusual. In the homestead he began his search in the common room and then proceeded in a U-shaped pattern. Thankfully, the interior was sparse—small beds with iron headboards and quilts, a few antique photos on the wall and tools near the back of the structure.

Footsteps stomped up the porch steps. "I forgot about the smoke shed out back," she called out. "Be back in a few minutes."

"Wait. I'll go with you." Dylan temporarily abandoned his search. Plenty of time for more of that before it grew dark.

"That's not necessary," she said as he joined her at the front.

"I insist."

They walked side by side, Ace scurrying along, nose to the ground. Only Bailey carried a metal detector to search the small smokehouse.

"Where is it? I don't recall ever seeing it before."

"It's a good thirty yards behind the house. We

stopped maintaining a path out there and keeping up the building. It's just another empty, dilapidated structure. A wonder it didn't burn to the ground in 2011."

The great fire of 2011 had raged through almost three-quarters of Okefenokee. Burned bark remained on many of the surviving trees and bore testimony to the devastation. But it hadn't been the first severe fire in the swamp's 6,500-year existence, and it wouldn't be the last. Incredibly, the marshland forest always regenerated and endured.

Saw palmetto and other shrubs encroached on the almost-forgotten path, and they proceeded single file until the small leaning shed was suddenly before them. Bailey went straight to the door and started inside.

At a swish of movement from above, Dylan glanced up, expecting to find a startled bird. But it was no bird. In fact, it was no bird or animal, or anything found in nature. The object missiling down toward Bailey was a homemade contraption—a large rock encased with rope and metal spikes protruding in every direction. It hung high on a nearby tree branch that must have been loaded with a trip-wire trigger.

The spiked rock hurtled with frightening speed. Its trajectory would blindside Bailey in her head and neck area. His mouth opened to scream, but there was no time for even that verbal warning. Another two seconds and the sharp spikes would pierce her unprotected, unsuspecting face. The blow could prove lethal.

Dylan lunged, desperate to save her. He propelled forward, watched as the stirring and hissing of air finally warned Bailey of danger and she looked up to determine its cause—a second too late for her to register the danger and respond.

He had to reach her. His arms grabbed at the empty space between them and then, finally, he felt her, latching on for dear life as they toppled to the sandy soil just in time to miss the spiked rock that swung toward them.

"What the heck was that?" Bailey asked in a whoosh of breath.

The rock crested a few yards upward, and then the pendulum swung toward them again. "Stay down," he cautioned.

Dylan rolled on his left side and immediately withdrew his sidearm, scanning the darkness between the trees. Was the killer still out there? Waiting and watching?

Logic told him no one lurked nearby unseen and unheard—that the purpose of the booby trap was to scare off trespassers when he wasn't around to guard the area.

"Another body might be nearby," Bailey whispered. "Either that, or Amy could be imprisoned not far from here."

"We have no proof, but that's my guess as well. Such an extreme measure is the mark of a dangerous person."

"Don't call for backup," she urged. "If he was close, he'd have already shot us. If you call, we've lost our chance to catch him unawares."

"I'm not calling," he assured her. "I want to get that bastard tonight as much as you do."

"What should we do about the booby trap? Tie it back up? If he sees it down, he'll guess the area's been compromised."

"At this point, I want him to know we're closing in. If we're lucky, he'll panic and make a stupid mistake. May I borrow your knife?"

"I've got this." Bailey took out her knife and made quick work of cutting the rope and freeing the attached weapon.

"Let's make a run for the cabin," he suggested. "I've already been in there. It's safe. We can search the shed in the morning."

They rose to their feet and he took out his gun again. "Stay close to me so that I'm free to shoot if needed. Stay close to me," he cautioned.

And then they were running. Despite that, it seemed to take twice as long on the return trip as it had on the initial foray. At the end of the trail, he held out an arm, stopping her from advancing into the clearing.

Dusk had soundlessly slipped into the wilderness, sprinkling long, distorted shadows in its wake. Birds loudly chirped as they flitted from tree to tree, seeking lofty asylum for their nightly rest. Nothing appeared out of the ordinary.

"Ready to make a quick break for the back door?" he asked.

"Ready."

Gun still drawn and at the ready, he burst from the tree line. Once Bailey ran past him, he dropped in behind her, shielding her as best he could. They tumbled inside, breathing hard.

"Stay down and away from the windows while I lock the front door."

Quickly, he slid the lock into place and did a quick walk-through of the rooms, thankful for the sparseness of the homestead. There were no closets to hide in, and the quilts were neatly tucked into the bottom of every mattress.

They were alone.

As though of one mind, they each sank to the floor and leaned their backs against a wall, catching their breaths. Dylan holstered his gun.

Bailey ran a trembling hand through her hair. "Thank you. If you hadn't been there, I could have been killed."

And if she'd been by herself and survived, the

killer would have found her before anyone else. Alone and defenseless, she'd have been easy prey as his next victim.

At a sudden clap of thunder, they both scrambled to their feet. "Just a summer storm rumbling in the distance," he said. He took her hand and squeezed it. "Sure you want to stay the night? If we do, we'll both need to be alert and on the lookout every second."

"Positive," she assured him. "I'm up for it. My insomnia can once again prove useful. It's no big deal for me to stay awake."

Confusion furrowed his brow. "I didn't know you struggled with insomnia. And what do you mean by it can help you *again*?"

"Forget it."

"No. Tell me, Bailey. Like I've said, I want to know everything about you."

"Just that…staying awake, or sleeping really light, keeps you alert for danger."

"What danger?" Sudden realization lit his mind. "Are you talking about your foster father?"

A grim smile tugged the edges of her mouth. "Never knew when a ticking time bomb like him would explode. I learned to stay prepared."

Anger rushed through him anew at the idea of Bailey being subjected to the likes of Edgar Slacomb. When this was over… "He'll pay for what he did to you," Dylan vowed. "And whoever you went to for help that ignored you."

He pulled her tightly against his chest, wishing like heck he could have protected her back then.

"Be careful what you wish for," she whispered in his ear.

He held her at arm's length. "What's that supposed to mean?"

"Never mind. I shouldn't have said anything." She shrugged out of his arms. "Shouldn't we each take a position by the windows to keep watch? We're on a stakeout. Remember?"

"The sooner you tell me who dropped the ball on helping you back then, the sooner we can do our job."

"Let it go."

"Tell me his name."

They eyed one another warily in the weight of the darkness, thunder rumbling ominously in the distance. Uneasiness danced under his veins. Whoever it was, Dylan had a feeling he wasn't going to like her answer.

"If you insist. The man I placed all my hope and trust in all those years ago was your father. Officer Dylan Armstrong Senior."

Chapter Twelve

The slash of incredulity and pain on Dylan's face made Bailey wish she could take back the words. It wasn't Dylan's fault that his dad was such a jerk. "It doesn't matter now," she hastened to add. "Ancient history."

"You're mistaken," he said at last, his voice harsh. "Dad would never stand by and let an innocent child suffer."

Her own anger, always on a slow simmer when she recalled the past, came bubbling to the surface. If Armstrong Senior had only made one little phone call, or filed an official report, she'd have been spared two more years of misery. Was that little bit of effort on his part too much trouble? It would have taken such a small part of his day to investigate the matter and have her removed from the foster family. But he'd done nothing.

"All I can tell you is that I went to your father and told him what was happening in that house. He said he'd get in contact with my social worker and take care of it immediately. So I went home and waited. And waited. Nothing ever came of it."

"No way. He—"

"Actually, I take that back. Something *did* happen. Edgar found out that I'd tried to turn him in and the situation got worse."

"How did he find out?"

"He never said. I certainly didn't tell him. Only two people knew of that conversation. Me." She paused a heartbeat. "And your dad."

"I'm going to get to the bottom of this," Dylan assured her. "Because my dad was one of the kindest people you'd ever want to meet."

"Was?" she asked uncertainly, immediately noticing his use of the past tense.

"He died over a decade ago."

Now she *really* wished she'd kept her mouth shut about the whole thing. If she'd known the senior Armstrong was dead she wouldn't have spoken ill of the man. Not to his son, anyway.

"Um, sorry, Dylan. Forget I said anything." She pointed at the windows. "Guess we should get to work. Right?"

Without waiting for a reply, she strode to the front window and pulled the homespun cotton curtain back an inch. Ace settled at her feet, resting his head on top of her shoes.

More blackness had descended over the swamp, and from far off, lightning slashed the inky sky. Every flash created a strobe-like effect that lit the landscape for a split second before it pitched dark again.

All the better to catch a killer.

Between the lightning and a nearby parking lot light up the road, she'd be able to detect anyone moving around the homestead. And Dylan had her back—in more ways than one. Funny how strange life could be. She'd gone all in trusting the son of the man she hated almost as much as Edgar Slacomb.

Should she tell Dylan? He might be in no mood to hear that she trusted him in spite of his father. She glanced over her shoulder where Dylan's long, lean body was silhouetted against the back window. She swallowed hard, remembering the feel of lying against that naked body, of his touch and his kisses that'd kept her up most of the night—in the best way possible, of course.

"See anything?" she called out softly.

"No."

Was he angry with her? Sulking perhaps? She tried again. "What's our game plan if we see somebody?"

"Tell me if you do. I'll call for backup before I leave the cabin to investigate."

"I'll go with you," she volunteered.

"You may be on loan to the sheriff's office for this investigation, but you're no cop. Don't even think about leaving the homestead if I venture out."

Ouch. He was definitely upset about her revelation. "Don't be angry, Dylan," she said softly. "If I'd known your father was dead, I wouldn't have told you."

He waited so long to answer that she thought he'd spend the rest of the night ignoring her. She kept her gaze focused on the front yard, a ball of misery knotting her gut.

"Don't ever apologize for speaking the truth," he said at last. "Or, rather, the truth as you see it. But I know my dad. He wouldn't have ignored a cry for help. There must be some logical explanation and I'll find out why."

"Fine with me." Her fingers curled tightly on the window ledge. Let him have his delusions on that score. She'd never bring up the subject again. The past had hurt her enough without it ruining her future as well. But would this issue always remain between them? She definitely wanted Dylan to be a part of her future.

That scared her more than whatever might be lurking in the darkness. Could she completely let go of her resentment toward his beloved father?

This case would be wrapping up soon, possibly even tonight. She didn't want it to end on a low note with Dylan. Silence slid between them again, but this time it was comfortable and not the previous tension-filled quiet.

Bailey concentrated on observing the dark edges that shadowed the small pool of available light, searching for any shift of light or movement. From the half-opened window, she listened to the high-pitched buzzing of myriad insects and the low thrumming of frogs, the night orchestra of the swamp. Her legs grew heavy, so she pulled a wooden chair close to the window and sat. At least until its hard surface became unbearable and she stood again to shake out her legs.

"Want to switch sides? Break up the monotony a bit?" Dylan offered.

"Might as well."

Without explanation, Dylan left the room, and then she heard a loud scraping of metal against the old wooden floorboards. He emerged in the common room, dragging a single-wide bed by its iron headboard.

"This'll be more comfortable than your chair," he said, sliding the bed under the rear window frame.

Gratefully, she sank onto the mattress. It was bumpy and hard, but infinitely better than the wooden chair.

"Heavenly," she said, shooting him a grateful smile.

He planted an unexpected, hot kiss on the top of her scalp before moving to the front window and settling in.

Smiling in bemusement, Bailey focused her attention on the backyard. The view here was much darker than the front. All she could make out was a subtle shift between the raked Chesser property and the looming tree line a good twenty yards away. The sliver of moonlight through the clouds was little help.

Another strobe of lightning flashed, illuminating the landscape in a brief, quick burst. A slight fluctuation of darkness darted at the right edge of the property. What was that? Bailey's heartbeat accelerated as she focused on the spot, waiting for another flash of lightning. She stared so hard and so long her eyes dried uncomfortably, but she had to be ready for the next bolt or she'd blink and miss the opportunity.

Lightning flashed again, but this time she spotted nothing unusual. A false alarm then. No point in having Dylan investigate. Thunder rumbled seconds later—the storm was moving closer. Leaves rustled in a sudden wind gust, and she smelled the scent of rain only seconds before it pounded the tin roof, a staccato percussion that drowned out all other sound. Rain splattered the window ledge, and she reluctantly closed the window. A shuffle and click from behind and she realized Dylan had done the same.

"So much for hearing anyone moving around out there," she quipped.

"This'll pass soon enough."

And well she knew it. These sudden Southern storms were violent—but often brief. "At least we have cover."

The pounding rain continued, lending a cozy atmosphere to the homestead where they were sheltered. Then she ruined the peaceful interlude, imagining Amy Holley alone in some damp hovel while the rain beat down and wondering when her abductor would return—when he'd kill her as he'd done to her sister. Did Amy imagine each day would be her last? Perhaps, at this point, the woman welcomed death.

The rain stopped as suddenly as it had begun, and she cracked the window, gulping in the soaked air. Time flowed effortlessly by, seconds, then minutes, then hours. Bailey's eyelids felt as though they lifted one-pound weights. She rubbed at the grittiness in her eyes, closed them a moment, and opened them again.

Blue eyes speared her with glittering hatred, only inches from her face—the window pane a fragile barrier between her and madness. Rain blurred his features, which only served to highlight the burning eyes. A scream tore through the cabin—her own, she realized belatedly. Ace growled and began barking.

Dylan was at her side. "Where is he?"

She lifted a finger to point, but only darkness pooled before them. "He—he was right here in front of the window a moment ago."

Dylan raced to the door and jerked it open. Ace shot outside and ran toward the woods. Dylan raised his gun and shot into the air. "Halt! Police officer."

She hurried to his side, peering over his shoulder. "Do you see anyone?"

"No. Get the flashlight." She picked it up from the table where he'd placed it earlier and turned it on, directing the beam along the back wall of the house.

There was no one.

Had she imagined the face? Perhaps she'd fallen asleep for an instant and had awakened from a nightmare.

"Maybe I imagined it," she said sheepishly.

"No. Ace saw or heard something, too. I'm going to try and follow. Lock yourself inside."

He ignored her protest, slipping into the night. She couldn't see him; she only heard his footsteps running across the yard. Bailey hurried back inside and grabbed the other flashlight. She stepped outside, aiming the elliptical beam at the tree line, but Dylan had disappeared. Damn it, she must have fallen asleep for the intruder to have managed to walk almost right up on her before she spotted him. If anything happened to Dylan, the fault would fall on her own shoulders.

At the back wall, she aimed the flashlight by the window and found footprints right under the sill. Someone *had* stood there. He knew her now, had seen her up close. He probably knew who she was from the first time she'd spotted him leaving the church, if it was the same man. Yet she still didn't know who he was.

Think, Bailey. What did you see at the window?

The eyes had magnetized her, commanding her complete attention. But what about the rest of his face? His hair? She replayed his image, but all she conjured were the crazy eyes and wet hair plastered on his skull.

Bailey stood on the steps, waiting. She withdrew her knife and wished like heck it was a gun. Where was Dylan? What was taking so long? She'd give him five minutes. If he hadn't returned, she'd call for backup.

A shout emanated from somewhere in the marsh. Dylan calling for Ace. Relief swooshed through her body. He was safe, at least at this moment. The air shifted from black to gray, the rising sun a sickly whisper of light in the east.

Ace broke through the underbrush, and she could swear he wore a look of frustration on his normally cheerful face. He wanted a piece of the guy he'd chased. Badly. Any other night, he might have caught his prey, but his injury had slowed him down too much. Again, this was entirely her fault. Dylan hadn't brought along a fresh, different tracking dog out of consideration for her fear.

Seconds later, Dylan strode through the woods and walked toward her.

"Did you see him?" she called out.

"Not a thing. I heard rustling ahead of me, but never saw anyone. Could have been a deer for all I know."

Her shoulders sagged in defeat. "I'm sorry."

"For what?"

"Everything. For not wanting backup this evening, for falling asleep, for having a dog with us who isn't at full running capacity."

"Whoa, there. Stop beating yourself up. I went along with the decision not to call last night. Remember?"

"But we were so close," she said with a groan. "He was right here, and I let him get away. Now we've got nothing."

"I wouldn't say that." He shone his flashlight by the wall. "We've got footprints. That's a start.

We'll make casts of them. Should provide us with general information about his size."

"Big whoop. You're just trying to make me feel better."

He came to where she stood and took a seat on the porch step. "Might as well sit a spell and watch the sunrise," he said, pointing to the empty space beside him. "Our guy won't venture back here anytime soon. I'll call the office shortly to report our findings and tell them they'll need to bring dogs with them."

Cadaver dogs to perhaps find Mary Thornton's body. She dropped down onto the wooden step, and Ace plopped at her feet, still panting from his recent exertion. They sat together, silently watching as the gray brightened in slow degrees and the rising sun's rays cast a coral glow on the clouds.

An owl hooted and the hairs on her arms rose.

"An owl's bad luck," she commented, absently fiddling with her necklace. "Some Native Americans believe they foretell death. I have a bad feeling about all this. Like the killer has unfinished business and there'll be more victims."

"Superstitions. Your friend's been filling your head with too many old tales."

"Maybe. But Lulu can be downright uncanny about signs. She sometimes predicts local news headlines before they're even reported."

"Coincidence," he said firmly. He nudged her shoulder playfully. "Next thing I know you'll be claiming to believe in the existence of the South Georgia Pig Man and the Skunk Ape."

"Who knows what lurks out there?" she said, attempting a laugh. "I've seen some pretty eerie things like balls of fire that glow—"

"Swamp gas."

Bailey cast him an enigmatic smile. His pragmatism didn't rankle. She had her own beliefs and he had his. She'd spent so much time alone in the wilderness that she could appreciate its mystery. At times, she'd sensed the ghosts of Native Americans striding through the land, had vividly imagined them as well as the desperate plight of slaves on the run, plus a host of other frantic people seeking to meld into the Okefenokee and become invisible to the rest of the world.

"Guess I'll head on inside and radio my boss," Dylan said, rising to his feet. "It will be light enough soon for forensics to sweep the area and others can begin searching."

"Join you in a minute," she answered, wanting a minute alone to sort her thoughts. The land spread before her, vast and unspoiled. Untamed. A morning mist blurred the sharp edges of the cypress and pine. In the muted black-and-green panorama, a white bird exploded from the underbrush, fluttering like an omen. She'd have to ask Lulu what it meant.

Bailey had a hunch it wouldn't be anything of a cheery nature.

Chapter Thirteen

It didn't take the cadaver dogs long.

The woods beyond the homestead echoed with the sounds of their barks and officers shouting harsh commands.

"They've found another one," Jeff commented beside him.

Dylan had expected as much, yet the commotion twisted his gut. "It's my guess it will be Mary Thornton's body," he said. "We found jewelry last night—I mean this morning—that may have belonged to her."

Jeff darted him a sharp side-glance. "Better get your timing straight when you speak to the boss. If you found it last night, you should have reported it immediately."

"Right. Of course, I would have called earlier," Dylan deadpanned.

"Whatever you say." His old friend wasn't fooled. Jeff's gaze drifted to where Bailey and

Evan stood off to the side. "The body y'all found on Billy's Island has been positively identified."

"Who?"

"Lisa Shaw."

He wasn't surprised. Dylan continued to stare at Bailey and Evan. From the set of their faces, the conversation looked intense. He hoped Bailey held firm to their story that they'd found the claddagh early this morning. Once again, Ace tried to wander off in Bailey's direction, but Dylan snapped his fingers for him to heel.

"What's going on between you and Ranger Covington?" Jeff asked.

"Nothing," he protested. Perhaps too vehemently. He lowered his voice and spoke more calmly. "We're working a case together. Period."

"Uh-huh. Be careful, that's all I'm saying."

Was it that obvious he had feelings for Bailey? "Point taken," he said stiffly.

Jeff clapped his shoulder. "I've known you too long. Probably no one else has caught wind. Not yet, anyway."

Time to change the subject. "What do you know about Evan Johnson?" Dylan asked his friend.

"The park manager? Not much really. He goes to the same church as my parents, so they'd know him better than me. I'll tap them. Why? You think he has something to do with the murders?"

Dylan wasn't ready to voice his suspicions, not even to Jeff. His annoyance with the man's advances to Bailey could well be coloring his perception of Evan's character.

"The man's probably above reproach. Let's just say that anyone with knowledge and opportunity should be closely looked at."

"Agreed."

"Did you ever get a chance to see if Bailey— er, Ranger Covington—had any mention in our records?"

"I poked around. There's nothing. Should there be?"

"If there was, it would have been over a decade ago. How far back do we keep paper files?"

"We don't. Old records are on microfilm in the government storage facility near Folkston." Jeff's forehead creased in concern. "What's going on, Dylan? You've been awful cryptic lately. I'll grant that your ranger is one hot chick, but don't be stupid. If she's trouble, better put it all out in the open. Think of your career."

"It's nothing that *she's* done wrong. It's what's been done against her, or rather, something that wasn't done for her. It's complicated." Dylan wouldn't betray Bailey's trust by spilling secrets, not even to his best friend.

Four officers, two on each side, carried a body bag into the backyard, where a forensics vehicle awaited it for transport to their lab. A respectful hush fell over the crowd of men and women until the car pulled out with its gruesome cargo.

Dylan caught Bailey's eyes. Dark circles stood out on her pale face and she hugged her arms tightly around her body. Witnessing a body recovered from a crime scene wasn't easy for anyone, least of all a civilian. That, coupled with lack of sleep, was obviously affecting her mentally and physically. Too often, he forgot that she was a civilian. Bailey was so good at providing leads and so determined in seeking justice that it was easy to forget this wasn't her everyday job.

He scooped Ace up and handed him to Jeff. "Take care of the little guy. He's had a long night, too."

"But—"

"Later, Jeff," he said, stepping in Bailey's direction and leaving the squirming pup in his friend's hands.

He didn't make it three steps before Sheriff Chesser intercepted him. "Anything you're not telling me? You and Ranger Covington sure got a lot accomplished in the first light of dawn—found the jewelry, cut down a trip wire and spotted footprints by the homestead back wall."

"Busy morning," he cryptically agreed.

Chesser narrowed his eyes, hands on his hips. "Odd how evidence keeps turning up whenever

Ranger Covington's around. She seems to have a real knack for finding things in the most obscure areas."

"She'd have made an excellent detective," Dylan said, pretending not to catch the sheriff's drift. "Too bad her calling was in forestry and not law enforcement."

"Even odder that only she's seen the suspected killer."

Dylan's voice grew sharp. "What are you saying?"

"If we hadn't found the remains of two women, I'd have said she was leading us on a merry chase."

"The bodies say otherwise."

"Which leads me to wonder how deep her involvement really is. Could she possibly be in league with the killer?" Chesser's eyes roamed to where Bailey and Evan continued their animated discussion.

"That's ridiculous," he said. Heat flushed the back of his neck and face. "If you want to cast suspicion on Evan Johnson, welcome to the club. But Bailey Covington? No way. Why would she cover for him if he's a killer?"

"Love—or lust—is a powerful motivator. I've seen the way Johnson looks at her when he thinks no one's watching. I mean, look at them even now. Their conversation looks too intense, not professional in the least."

"That's probably because Johnson is putting another unwanted move on her."

"Another one?"

"This wouldn't be the first time. I better head over and check it out."

"So now you're playing her protector, are you?"

"She's a colleague," he said tightly.

Bailey happened to break her gaze with Johnson and their eyes met. She quirked a brow as though to ask if everything was okay on his end. He gave a curt nod before giving the sheriff his full attention again.

"Make sure your relationship with Covington stays professional," Chesser warned him. "Keep your eyes open and remember this conversation. If I get wind of any hanky-panky, you'll be stuck at a desk the rest of your career. Understood?"

He wanted nothing more than to tell his boss where to go, but he couldn't risk getting pulled from the case. "Yes, sir. Are we done here?"

"We are."

Dylan quickly made his way to Bailey and Evan Johnson, conscious of Chesser watching every step he took.

"Done filling your boss in on our findings?" he asked Bailey while holding Johnson's gaze, not bothering to address him directly or extend any courtesy. Johnson had lost his respect.

"I am. Just need to report to headquarters and fill out paperwork." She nodded toward Johnson. "I'll be at the office shortly."

He followed Bailey and they made their way across the homestead.

"I imagine you have even more reports to fill out than I do," she said. "Going to be a long day for both of us. Everything okay with your boss?"

"I was going to ask you the same thing. You and Johnson looked…engrossed."

Bailey crinkled her nose. "He's upset with all the negative publicity."

"Chesser mentioned that the annual astronomy night was canceled for this evening. I know staff has put in a lot of time to arrange for teachers to speak to the public about the stars but they really had no choice, big event or not."

"Not to mention all the telescopes we've already arranged to bring in for everyone," Bailey said. "Speaking of your boss, y'all seemed to be having your own intense conversation."

"He's in a tight spot, too. Between the press and the feds coming in and assuming control of the case—"

"The FBI's in charge now?" She stopped in her tracks and regarded him with wide eyes.

"Yeah, multiple bodies will do it."

"What about us? Will we continue working together?"

From the corner of his eye, Dylan spotted several people glancing their way. He needed to remember that they were both going to be closely scrutinized from here on out.

"Honestly, I can't say for sure." He cocked his head to the side. "Let's keep walking. We seem to have an audience."

Once they hit the sandy path to the parking lot, he turned to her. "You may not have noticed, but we're being watched."

"But why? We're the only ones who've made any kind of break in the investigation."

"Exactly."

At her quizzical scowl, he shrugged and tried to explain. "Cops are a suspicious bunch. Too many breaks or leads and they wonder if the person or persons providing them have their own agenda."

"They think we had something to do with those poor women?" Her voice was loud, and he feared it might carry to the others.

"Let's talk about it in my car."

"But what about Ace? What about all our things? We can't just leave them—"

He laid a hand on her arm and gently pulled her forward. "I'll have Jeff take care of everything. We have a long afternoon ahead. I don't know about you, but I'll be ready to crash after the administrative work is finished. Tomorrow, we'll figure out where we go from here."

"Makes sense," she agreed. "But I'd hate to be bumped off the case when everything's finally heating up."

"Hadn't we run out of options, anyway? There aren't any other places in the swamp with standing structures located near a shrine of some sort."

"Not that I can think of," she admitted, running a hand through her chestnut hair. "But I can't give up trying. I'll rack my brain and see if I can come up with another location to check."

"Theoretically, Clay Slacomb could still be our guy. Whoever came by the cabin might be a Peeping Tom or something. I know the odds of that are slim, but it's something everyone will keep in mind."

"They can think what they want, but I no longer believe either of the Slacombs is guilty. I didn't recognize that man at the window."

They slipped into his car, and he started the engine, willing the air-conditioning to quickly kick in. He leaned back in the seat and Bailey did the same. Cold air blasted through the vents and cooled his clammy face and forearms.

"Heaven," he said after a minute. "I could probably doze off right here, right now."

"Me, too," she admitted, flashing him a wan

smile. "Matter of fact, the AC's made me so mellow I can't even muster the energy to stay angry at Sheriff Chesser."

"What do you mean?"

"That's who you were talking to before me. So if anyone's raised suspicions about us, or me, it's your boss."

"He's a stickler for protocol and jaded from years on the job."

"Ha. Maybe he should cast aspersions on his own self. He has knowledge and opportunity. Heck, his family is connected to the Chesser homestead where a body's been found."

"Hmm," he answered noncommittally, pulling out of the parking lot and entering the main road. It felt good to be behind the wheel and return to some degree of normalcy. "How about some coffee?"

"Do you even need to ask?"

He took her hand and brought it to his mouth, bestowing a quick kiss on her knuckles. "No matter what happens with our jobs, I still want to see you, Bailey."

His breath caught when she didn't answer straightaway. "Bailey?" he asked huskily.

She closed her eyes and leaned her head back. "I'd like that," she said, so softly he almost didn't hear it.

His shoulders slumped with a release of tension he hadn't even known he carried.

His phone vibrated in his pocket, an urgent, angry command to pick it up. Dylan fished it out and pressed a button. "Armstrong here."

"There's been another missing person reported," Sheriff Chesser barked without preamble. "Forget the reports and turn around. We need you back. Both of you."

Energy spiked his tired muscles and he did a swift U-turn as he flipped on his siren. All thoughts of a quiet afternoon sipping coffee and writing reports fled out the window.

A sea of strobing blue lights approached as a convoy of state trooper vehicles sped by his car.

"What in the world's happened?" Bailey asked. "Did they find another body buried on the property?"

"A new person's been reported missing. I don't know the details yet."

"And here I thought we'd scared the killer into hiding. I was so sure we were close to capturing him before someone else got hurt."

"Ditto. Never can tell about these kinds of cases though."

"I'm assuming Clay Slacomb's definitely off the suspect list now. Unless he managed to escape from county lockup?"

"No. Chesser would have told me if that's the case."

The minute he stopped in the parking lot, they both raced down to the homestead, where they found Chesser, Johnson and a few FBI agents stood at the picnic table by the edge of the property. The place was crawling with law enforcement officers and dogs. Between the sirens, officers barking orders and the buzzing of two-way radios, Dylan's ears rang. At the picnic table, a large map of the Okefenokee wildlife refuge lay open. Black X's marked the spots where bodies were found and the trophy pieces located.

"Who's missing?" Dylan asked as he took a seat.

"A woman named Janet Blackwell. Husband called because she never returned from her all-night factory shift in Beulah. We're searching all roads between there and her home in Folkston. Jeff and a couple of feds are going to speak with the husband." Chesser turned to Bailey. "Any ideas on where we might narrow our search?"

Indignation burned in Dylan's gut. First Chesser threw aspersions against Bailey for her hunches and now he wanted her help?

Bailey shook her head. "Honestly, no. But let me think." She scanned the map, running a hand through her hair. "There's a couple sheds on Gannet Lake and over by Buzzard's Roost.

Could be there are mounds around there, too, but I don't recall. What about you, Evan? Do you remember?"

"I'm not sure either."

Dylan wanted to snort. Some help her boss was.

Bailey turned back to Chesser with a shrug. "Sorry I can't help more this time."

The sheriff gave a curt nod. "Thought it was worth a shot to ask."

"If you're through with us?" Evan asked. "Ranger Covington needs to file a report on all this."

Chesser waved a dismissive hand at Evan and Bailey. "Y'all are free to go. You, too, Armstrong. We've got more than enough officers to start the new search."

"I'd rather stay and join in. If you don't mind, sir."

Now that Bailey had planted a seed of suspicion about the sheriff, he wouldn't feel right unless he kept an eye on how Chesser handled this latest development.

A woman's life depended on it.

Chapter Fourteen

Bailey emailed her report to Evan, leaned back in her chair and gazed out the kitchen window of her cabin. The first hint of dusk smudged the sky. She should be tired but a second wind, largely the result of several cups of coffee, energized her body, so she stood and paced. What was the latest news on the missing woman? So far, she'd refrained from calling Dylan to check, but now curiosity overrode concern of interrupting his work.

She sent him a text and then carried her phone to the porch. For her, the best remedy for restlessness was quiet time outside. Much as she wanted to enjoy the respite, her mind kept circling back to the missing women. Was Amy still alive after all this time? Every day that passed, the hope of finding her grew smaller. And if the killer had captured another woman, it might mean Amy was dead and he craved a new victim to replace the old.

A police car rumbled down her road—way too early for the sporadic drive-by patrol of her cabin. A flutter of unease danced inside her chest until she saw it was Dylan. He pulled into the driveway and held up his phone as he exited his car. "Just got your text."

"You didn't have to come see me in person to answer it," she teased.

"Maybe I needed an excuse to see you." He plopped down beside her and pressed a quick, hot kiss on her lips.

"Any news?"

"Nothing definite, but we discovered that Mrs. Blackwell is having an affair with a coworker. Who also happens to be AWOL. Chances are pretty good that we'll find they've run off together. Troopers put out an APB on the guy's car, so I'm hoping this is wrapped up soon."

She closed her eyes and released a quick breath. If the killer hadn't struck again, it might bode well for Amy. *Hang in there, Amy.* She leaned in to Dylan as he threw an arm over her shoulder and gave her a brief hug.

"I still don't know where to search in the morning," she admitted. "Before I waste anyone's time, I thought I'd go out on my own and poke around Buzzard's Roost and Gannet Lake."

"We'll go together. Your guess is as good as anybody's at this point."

"Not sure your boss will like the idea."

"Speaking of which… We need to be careful about our, uh, relationship. Chesser warned me to keep it professional."

"So did Evan." She looked up at him. "I hope this new directive doesn't mean you won't spend tonight with me."

His eyes darkened to a deep green and he leaned his forehead against hers. "I'd like nothing better, but it won't do for my vehicle to be spotted by whatever officer patrols here tonight." He straightened with a sigh of regret. "Besides, you must be worn out. You need uninterrupted sleep."

She'd much rather have Dylan's lovemaking interrupting that sleep, but she kept the thought to herself.

"I am concerned about you, though. That man last night got a really good close-up of your face. And given the fact someone already tried to burn down your cabin—well, you see why I'm worried."

"I'm not too thrilled with the idea of being alone, either," she admitted.

"Why don't you stay with your friend down the road?"

Bailey glanced over at Lulu's empty driveway. "She's not even home. Holt's in town so she might be staying at his place."

"Holt's her boyfriend?"

"Yeah. Holt Rucker. His job keeps him on the road a good bit. I don't want to be a third wheel there."

"Why don't you call her? If she's not going to be home, you could sleep at her house. Our guy won't know to check there."

Bailey hesitated. It went against the grain to ask a favor from anyone, but this was Lulu after all. Her friend wouldn't mind a bit. "Okay."

"Go ahead and call her. I can let the patrol officer know where you'll be, and I'll leave here reassured you'll be okay."

She called Lulu, and her friend answered almost at once. Bailey asked about spending the night, and Lulu immediately agreed.

"But I have an even better idea," Lulu said. "Holt's hitting the road shortly. Got a last-minute gig in Maggie Valley when the scheduled guide canceled. Why don't you spend the night over here with me at his place? Would be safer for both of us than my cabin."

Guilt pinged Bailey's gut. She hadn't even considered that her request would put Lulu in possible danger. "Of course. Text me his address and I'll be on my way."

"What's up?" Dylan asked as soon as she ended the call.

"Change of plans. I'm staying at her boyfriend's place tonight. Which should be even safer."

"Perfect." Dylan tapped on his phone and paused, fingers at the ready. "What's that address?"

Sighing, she reopened her phone and saw Lulu had already texted, so she read the address aloud. He was being overprotective, but it'd be easier to provide the information than get in an argument.

Dylan left shortly afterward, first planting another quick, hot kiss on her lips. Bemused, she packed an overnight bag and headed out. The rhythmic whir of car tires on the blacktop road lulled her into drowsiness. Her second wind had definitely fled. At least Lulu would understand her exhaustion and wouldn't expect to be entertained.

At the first fork in the road, she veered left as the GPS instructed. Ah, she knew this road well. It was the back way to Edgar Slacomb's house. Just her luck if Holt Rucker turned out to be the man's neighbor and best friend. If Edgar was over there, she'd drive right on by the house and make up an excuse to Lulu for not showing up as planned. She'd much rather spring for a motel room in the nearest city than suffer Edgar's company for one minute. No doubt he'd prefer to avoid her, too.

The road narrowed and made a sharp curve

to the right, and then sand replaced asphalt. According to her GPS, she had another quarter mile to go. She steeled herself for some messy, primitive cabin but was pleasantly surprised when she arrived at a neat ranch house with a well-tended vegetable garden on one side. Lulu stepped onto the porch and waved.

Two cars were parked in the curved drive—so Holt hadn't yet left.

"Any trouble finding this place?" Lulu called from the front porch.

"Nope. GPS is the best invention ever." In Bailey's directionally challenged mind, it even topped man's landing on the moon. She lifted her overnight bag from the passenger side and strode to the porch.

"Nice garden," she commented.

"Holt takes a lot of pride in it. When he's gone, I come out here and keep it watered for him. We've got corn, tomatoes, zucchini, cucumbers—all the essentials. Plus, I planted an herb patch. Once I made him a salad with fresh oregano and basil, he was hooked on herbs. Come on out and I'll show it to you."

Bailey dropped her bag on the porch swing and followed Lulu. She wasn't much into gardening, but her friend took pride in it. Dutifully, she went with Lulu down the rows, oohing over the size of the tomatoes. Not far from the garden, several bags of fertilizer and lime were stacked against the side of a potting shed.

She yawned and stretched her hands high in the air.

"Sorry, I'm rambling on and you're tired," Lulu said, coming to an abrupt halt. "Let's go inside. I saved you some leftovers from dinner. Barbecue ribs and mashed potatoes."

They drifted toward the house.

"When's Holt leaving?" She hated being a third wheel.

"Soon. He's packing his bags now. Ah, there he is."

Holt passed by them carrying a suitcase and several pressed uniforms in a plastic bag slung over one shoulder. Bailey glanced at the patch on one of the shirts, noting the words Southern Expeditions embroidered in a circle around a tree emblem.

"Evening, Bailey," he said. "Enjoy your stay. I'm a bachelor, but I generally keep things tidy 'round here."

"Your home's lovely," she assured him. "Thanks for letting me come over at the last minute."

"No trouble at all. Lulu will take good care of you. She told me you've had a rough week. I was sad to hear they'd found the body of one of them missing women." He paused on the steps and set down the suitcase. "Making any progress on that case?"

"A little, but I can't discuss the details."

"I understand. I read about Clay Slacomb's arrest but since another person went missing today, looks like y'all locked up the wrong man."

"Maybe. Maybe not."

Holt flashed a rueful grin. "I see I won't get any inside scoop from you."

"I bet that latest woman, Janet, turns up by morning," Lulu said.

Bailey whirled to face her. "How did you— I mean, what makes you say that?"

"Woman's intuition. They showed a photo of her on the TV, a pretty little woman, and then later reported that a coworker—a *male* coworker—had also gone missing. Easy to put two and two together."

"Then I say there's a good possibility Clay Slacomb is the killer," Holt said. "Everyone knows them Slacombs are nothing but trouble."

Bailey didn't rise to the bait and pointedly didn't respond.

"How about a cup of coffee before you hit the road?" Lulu asked him. "Long drive ahead."

"Sure thing. Be right there."

Holt continued to his car and Bailey picked up her overnight bag and followed Lulu inside. The decor was minimalistic, but cozy—all leather furniture and a slightly scarred coffee table and end tables.

"Nice place," she commented, tossing her bag on the sofa and following Lulu to the kitchen.

Pine cabinets and flooring glowed amber under the kitchen light, and the room smelled of tangy, sweet barbecue sauce.

"Here's a plate." Lulu pointed to a drawer by the sink. "Utensils in there. Want some iced tea?"

"Yes, thanks."

She loaded her plate with food and took a seat at the table, her gaze drifting to the garden. Unease snaked down her spine for no good reason.

Lulu set the iced tea on the table and then sat across from her. A fading ray of sunlight lit the gold chain around her neck and the cross pendant that dangled on her olive skin.

Bailey stared at the pendant—transfixed.

"Something wrong?" Lulu asked.

"That's a pretty necklace. But what happened to the turquoise and copper one you always wear?"

Lulu lifted a hand, her fingers caressing the golden charm. "Holt got me this."

"When?" Bailey's voice was sharp, shredding the short distance between them.

Lulu's hand abruptly dropped. "Weeks ago. Why? What's your problem?"

"Nothing. Never mind." She was being ridicu-

lous, making a federal case over a stupid necklace. This case was working a number on her.

Holt's boots clomped across the den and her
heart inexplicably pounded inside her chest.

"Reckon I'll take that coffee to go, Lulu. The
sooner I hit the road, the more shut-eye I'll catch
before the job."

Lulu immediately rose to fix his drink, and
Holt turned to her, his blue eyes probing and intense. Had he overheard their conversation? And
what would it matter if he did? All she'd asked
was when he'd given the necklace to Lulu.

She couldn't look away from those blue eyes.
A cabinet door opened and closed, and from her
peripheral vision, she observed Lulu pouring coffee into a thermos. Perfectly normal, everyday
kind of sounds. But Bailey's skin tingled, and her
ears whirred a warning that something was…*off.*

Way, way off.

"Here ya go," Lulu said, thrusting the thermos
into Holt's hands.

Holt smiled at Bailey. A curve of the lips that
had nothing to do with amusement. His eyes
were hard and cold.

Had they been the mad, mad blue eyes that
had glared at her last night in the rain? Or was
she the crazy one in the room?

Holt jerked his gaze from her to Lulu. "Walk
me to my car?" he asked.

The couple left the kitchen, *clomp clomp clomp*, through the den, then the screen door banged shut—loud as a shotgun blast in the middle of a quiet forest. And there she sat, mired in suspicion as her mind flickered with ominous images:

The round patch on his uniform embroidered with a tree—which reminded her of the drawing on the wooden flooring at Floyd's Island. *Click*.

Holt's acceptance and reverence of Lulu's relics the night he'd buried the old crow feather from her necklace. *Click*.

His intimate knowledge of the swamp. *Click*.

The cross pendant, same as the one missing from Amy, that he gave Lulu. *Click*.

A schedule and job where he came and went with no one questioning his movements. *Click, click, click, click* and *click*.

But did it all add up to a guilty man?

With shaky legs, Bailey rose from the table and peered out the kitchen window, watching as Lulu and Holt talked. The voices were low enough so that even with the open window, she couldn't make out the words.

Everything her brain fired off was so circumstantial, so flimsy—except for the necklace. Somehow, she had to convince Lulu to give her Holt's gift and let the cops check it out.

She watched as at the car, Holt suddenly pulled

Lulu into an embrace and they began to kiss. Bailey stepped away from the window and paced the room, trying to think of a reason to give Lulu for such an odd request. She couldn't outright accuse her boyfriend of anything. How insulting would that be? Lulu was a good friend, and asking for the necklace could ruin that friendship forever.

Think. There has to be a way.

A car engine started, and she returned to peer out the window. Holt's car puttered down the drive and out of sight. The wild beating of her heart slowed. At least he was gone. She'd sit down with Lulu and think of something. If she couldn't come up with an excuse, the truth would have to suffice.

Lulu returned to the kitchen, her face as calm and inscrutable as ever. "Let me refresh your drink. I made an herbal tea I think you'll like. It's got kava kava in it, which'll help you unwind. You seem a little tense tonight."

She didn't need tea. She needed that necklace. Bailey watched as Lulu boiled water and then poured it over crushed herbs before returning to the table and placing it in front of her. "Drink up and let's talk."

The boiled sludge didn't look terribly inviting. Grudgingly she took a small sip. Her mouth puckered. "Ugh. It's so bitter."

Wordlessly, Lulu got up and returned with a packet of sugar and a spoon. "This'll help."

Bailey stirred the tea and tried again. "Better. Look." She cleared her throat and plunged in. "Lulu, we have to talk. There's no easy way to broach this, so I'll just come right out and—"

"Finish your drink first. You sound distressed and this will help you relax."

She lifted the mug and scalding tea slushed over the brim. Why were her hands shaking so bad? Lulu would probably laugh at her strange request and hand over the necklace. If her friend got upset, she'd just get in her car and leave. Plenty of good motels down the road in Waycross. Bailey sipped until the mug was half empty and then set it down on the counter.

Or rather—she tried to. Her fingers and mouth were strangely numb. The mug wobbled in her hand, and Lulu steadied the trembling with a steady hold on her wrist.

"You haven't finished yet," she said.

Her friend's face distorted, as though she were looking at Lulu's face at the bottom of a pool of water. Something was wrong. A calm, inner voice that she remembered from long ago kicked in—the voice that guided her at the worst moments in foster care. It was clear as an unflawed diamond and spoke with an authority that brooked immediate action.

You're in danger. Do not drink another drop. Do not mention the necklace.

Bailey snapped her wrist. The mug fell on the table and then rolled onto the floor, breaking into shards that seemed to explode in slow motion. Black-green liquid sloshed on the table and spilled onto her shorts. "Oops," she said, as though it'd been an accident. "Sorry about that. I'll clean it up."

"I've got it."

They both stood, and Bailey forced a shaky laugh. "I'm wet. I better go change clothes."

"How are you feeling?" Lulu leaned forward, scrutinizing her face. "You look a little shaky."

She stepped back and fought to not betray her growing uneasiness. "I'm fine. Back in a minute."

Her legs were wobbly, but she stumbled forward and picked her overnight bag up off the sofa. She waved at Lulu and headed for the hallway, a fake, goofy grin plastered on her face. "Which room am I in?"

"Last one to the left."

She felt Lulu's eyes on her as she made it down the hallway and into the bedroom. Heart thudding, she locked the door behind her and leaned against it. *Deep breaths. Get it together and then scope out the area.*

The sparse room contained a double bed covered with a plaid comforter, a nightstand and one small dresser. More importantly—blessedly—it had a window on the back wall. Bailey flipped on the light switch and ripped into her bag, flinging clothes everywhere. Where the heck was her cell phone and car keys? She must have set them on the coffee table when she'd come in. She leaned her ear against the door.

A murmur came from the den. Lulu was on the phone. Talking with Holt perhaps? Ever so slowly, she eased open the door.

Lulu stood in front of the sofa, staring at her hand—which clutched Bailey's keys. Bailey stifled a groan. Those keys were her only means for a quick, certain escape. Only Lulu's profile was visible, and it shook her that the woman was so unemotional.

"I told you. She's out of it. I slipped something in her tea."

She spoke with a flatness that nonplussed Bailey more than if Lulu had ranted like a crazed psychopath thwarted from getting her way. Until ten minutes ago, she'd trusted this woman with her life. Her mind spun like a Ferris wheel on speed, until her inner voice nixed the buzzing in her ears.

So, she betrayed you. Deal with that fact later.

"Go ahead and circle on back," she heard Lulu say.

Get out now!

Quickly, Bailey shut the bedroom door and clicked the lock shut. That might buy her a precious minute to escape. She fled to the window and tried to lift the sash. It held tight. From a distance, footsteps started down the hallway. She pushed against the window with every scrap of her energy and it squeaked partially open with a begrudging protest.

The footfalls grew closer.

No time to fiddle with the screen fastenings. She kicked out the screen and then plunged forward headfirst. Her hips strained in the tight opening and she dangled from the window, half in and half out. A sharp rap sounded at the locked door.

"Bailey? You all right? What's going on in there?"

The doorknob violently rattled.

Chapter Fifteen

Bailey hit the ground on her right side with a hard thump. A combination of fear, fresh air and pain helped sober her from the worst effects of whatever Lulu had added to her drink. Yet when she stood on shaky legs, a bit of brain fog remained.

A splintering crash rent the air behind her. Lulu was kicking in the door and, from the sound of it, was about to burst into the room. Cursing herself one last time for not keeping her car keys and phone in her pocket, Bailey fled to the woods. There was no other option.

Her legs stumbled forward as though they were made of lead, her brain and muscles not quite connecting. A dangerous whirring buzzed through her brain and she bit her lip hard, concentrating on the pain to keep from passing out.

The full moon beamed on her like a spotlight as she ran to the trees.

"Bailey! Get back here! Why are you running?"

Lulu's screams felt like claws gouging down

her back. It was only when Bailey slipped into the shadows of the woods that she dared to look behind her.

Lulu stood at the window, her long black hair streaming in the wind and dark eyes burning like hot ash—like a witch from a childhood nightmare—and then she disappeared.

She's coming for me.

Blindly, Bailey moved forward a few feet. Her foot hit an exposed root and she tripped in the darkness. *Oomph.* Her forehead bumped against the rough, solid bark of a tree and the rest of her body shortly followed.

"Damn it," she cried, slapping a hand on her bleeding forehead.

Even with the full moon, the air was dark and thick. Bailey blinked, willing her eyes to adjust.

A door slammed from behind her, and she was still close enough to the house to make out the sound of Lulu running across the wooden porch.

Again, she started forward, her hands out in front of her to prevent running into another obstacle. Every step was methodical as she tested the ground an instant before each footfall.

She was getting nowhere fast.

"Baaay-leee! Where are you?"

An unexpected beam of illumination burst through the night, and it took Bailey a moment to realize Lulu was directing a flashlight into the woods. Soon, she'd be revealed like a possum stuck in the headlights—easy prey for Lulu and Holt. An effortless night's hunt for the killers.

She turned back in the direction of Holt's yard in time to see Lulu tuck a gun in the waistband of her pants. The lady meant business.

"I think there's been a misunderstanding," Lulu shouted. "Come back and let's talk."

Like heck. She may have been a blind fool all these years when it came to the true nature of her former friend, and she might still be a tad slow from Lulu's drug, but she wasn't an idiot. Bailey picked up her pace, frantic to put more distance between them. Leaves crunched underfoot, sounding as loud as firecrackers in the stillness. But she couldn't worry about the noise. Her focus was on moving forward as quickly as possible, careful not to fall and risk hurting an ankle or knocking herself out with another head injury.

An elliptical beam of light fractured through the shrubs and foliage, less than six feet to her right. Bailey sucked in her breath, and then took advantage of the sudden illumination to run forward several feet, stopping when the light arced away.

It happened twice more. The light illuminated a path for several precious seconds and then she'd dart forward, stopping and leaning her back against a tree when the beam moved on. Her eyes darted upward to the silver tops of the tree limbs etched against the moon. Maybe she should climb. Would Lulu think to shine the flashlight upward?

Bailey decided against it. She imagined herself being cornered while Lulu and Holt stood below, waiting with knives. Or they could shoot, picking her off like a bird.

So on she went. Sandy soil gave way to damp peat and the ground grew more wet as she forged ahead, her sneakers glopping in the mud. The tracks would make it easier for the killers to hunt her, but it couldn't be helped. Her legs grew weak with exhaustion and her stomach rumbled. She leaned against a tree and retched. Immediately, her stomach settled down, happy to have expelled whatever toxin she'd ingested in the tea. That over, Bailey continued forward, perhaps in circles as far as she knew.

Abruptly, the darkness lightened several degrees and she scanned a small clearing ahead. An old barn and a deserted, rusty tractor stood silhouetted at the far side of the open land. A bolt of recognition shot up her spine. She *knew* this place. Edgar Slacomb's house was less than a quarter mile to the east. Somehow, it brought a modicum of comfort to get her bearings.

Now what? She'd never make it to the barn undetected without the cover of trees and underbrush. She bent over double, panting hard and nursing a stitch in her side.

Lulu had gone off on a tangent, drifting further away, but the flashlight beam must have picked up her muddy footprints because she reversed direction and headed unerringly toward her.

She had maybe five minutes. Even if she made it to the barn, circling around the clearing using the cover of trees, Lulu would no doubt search the barn when she spotted it. *Think*. How could she cover her tracks? The image of a ditch formed in her memory, and she recalled one was located close by. Last night's rain had probably filled it with water. If she found it, she could run in the water, obliterating her footsteps.

It shaved at least two minutes of her precious time, but she located it and ran, water sloshing up to her knees. The trampling of leaves drew ever closer. Time was up.

Bailey dropped to the side of the narrow ditch, covering her body with mud, leaves and pine needles. Playing possum was her best bet. The wet peat absorbed her body like quicksand, which terrified and relieved her all at once. She lay absolutely still and tried to muffle her labored breathing, which sounded loud as a hurricane to her ears. A mosquito buzzed by her nose and she squinted her eyes closed, resisting the impulse to swat it away.

Twigs snapped, and bushes and low-lying tree limbs slapped against a moving object.

"Where'd she go?" Lulu grumbled, the flashlight beam casting a merciless light not ten yards from where she lay hidden.

Lulu tried to draw her out again. "I know you're nearby. Heard the water sloshing as you ran. Holt's not here, Bailey. Everything'll be all right. Come on out now. You know I won't hurt you."

Bailey didn't believe a word.

Loud sighs and muttered cursing ensued. Too late, she wished she'd confronted Lulu instead of running to the bedroom. She was younger and in better shape than Lulu and could have easily beat her in a fight. Clearly, the spiked tea had muddled her mind. And now it was too late. She couldn't out-muscle a gun.

"Damn it, girl," Lulu spat out. "You'd rather deal with me than Holt. I can promise you that."

A bit of mud seeped into Bailey's nose and a sneeze began to tickle. She gritted her teeth, fighting the urge. At last, the tickling stopped, and she breathed easier.

"Ahhh, that's more like it."

Slowly, Bailey turned toward the sound of Lulu's muttering. The woman eased down on the ground and sat back against a tree, the gun resting in her lap. Lulu killed the flashlight.

"If you strike out now in the dark, I'll hear you," she said in an almost cheerful voice. "Stay in your hidey-hole then. At first light of dawn, I'll be here waiting for you. And I *will* find you."

Bailey shivered in the slime, contemplating her options. No one would miss her tonight. Dylan thought she was safe spending the night with a trusted friend. By the time he tried to contact her in the morning and grew alarmed, it would be too late.

Dylan. What she wouldn't give to see him right now, to wrap her arms around him and lay her head against his broad chest and feel like everything was going to be all right, that she was safe and protected.

"Holt's my man, Bailey," Lulu continued in the same casual, conversational tone. "I'd do anything for him. Anything. I was dying living alone. I'm not some cold fish like you who doesn't care if she has a man or not."

Dying of loneliness? She'd never known, had always assumed Lulu was perfectly content with her solitary life, just as she had been with hers. Or rather, she'd thought she didn't want anyone. But Dylan had come into her life and proved her wrong on that count. She hadn't even realized how much she'd come to care for him until now.

"Sure, Holt's got his flaws. He likes to grab them young women and have his way. 'Course he has to kill them later or they'll identify him, ya see?"

Chills raced over every inch of her muddy body. Bailey kept her silence and wished Lulu would do the same. She didn't want to hear any more of the craziness.

A rustling erupted from somewhere behind Lulu and Bailey stifled her impulse to cry out.

Lulu scrambled to her feet. "Holt? That you?"

A doe and her fawn emerged and then gave a startled whistle before running back in the direction they'd come. Her heart slowed its wild beat. It wasn't Holt—not this time. But he'd be here eventually.

Lulu chuckled and resumed her spot leaning against a tree. As though reading Bailey's mind, she said, "Oh, you'll never escape Holt, hon. He's already disabled your car. I suspect he's hiding out somewhere near the house, figuring you'll come back and try to drive off or call for help. He'll keep an eye on the main road, too. He's almost as good at tracking as I am. If I don't return with you by dawn, he'll swing by here and help me handle this situation."

She chuckled again. "Seems I'm as forgetful as you when it comes to keeping up with my cell phone. If I had it, I could call, and he'd be here in minutes. Way I figure, he might get tired of waiting for you to show up at his place and start tracking. He could pop by anytime."

As if she wasn't in enough danger. Bailey reasoned that she had two choices. Wait for dawn and hope to catch Lulu unawares as she stepped close to her hiding place, or make a mad dash at her now. The disadvantage with option one was that Holt might show up and she'd be outnumbered and unable to take them both down. But the second option? There was a high probability that Lulu would shoot her before she could tackle her to the ground.

Lulu gave a loud yawn, stretching her legs out in front of her.

Which made Bailey realize she had a third option. Wait it out a bit longer. If luck was on her side, Lulu would fall asleep. She'd sneak up on her, get the gun and…shoot her? Could she really shoot another person? Bailey gritted her teeth. Whatever it took to escape alive, that's what she'd have to do.

Mind made up, she bided her time, thankful that Lulu had grown tired of being chatty. Instead, the woman moaned out a few more yawns.

I'll count to one hundred, Bailey decided. Whether Lulu was asleep or not, she'd make her move for freedom. Lying in the wet peat in a coffin-sized ditch, waiting for Holt to arrive, had become unbearable. Better to face a fatal shot in the chest than to be captured by Holt and endure a slower death.

…*forty-eight, forty-nine*, she silently counted. A snore rumbled nearby. Had her luck turned? Or was Lulu trying to fake her out? She'd find out soon enough. Bailey resumed counting, slow and deliberate, eyes and ears attuned to the pulse of the forest at night.

…*ninety-eight, ninety-nine*… Her breath grew shallow and her heartbeat accelerated…*one hundred*.

Eyes focused on Lulu, Bailey shifted slightly in the mud. She couldn't see Lulu's face in the darkness to tell if her eyes were even closed, but her head lolled to one side, her arms out to the side, palms up, and the revolver lay in her lap.

Mud trickled and splashed in the ditch as Bailey moved, but Lulu didn't react. Bailey strove for patience even as she longed to hurtle herself straight at Lulu. The closer she came to her enemy, the better her chances of taking her down.

She struggled to her knees, waited, then rose to her feet. A suctioning noise escaped as she lifted a foot. Still no movement from Lulu. Slowly, slowly, inch by inch, Bailey emerged from the ditch and made her way over. So very close now. Close enough to see Lulu's face. Her eyes were closed. Bailey crouched, advancing. A few more steps and she'd snatch the gun.

Whoo-whoo, an owl hooted from a nearby tree, and she nearly screamed. *Damn.*

Lulu awakened with a jerk and rose to her knees, wildly searching for the source of the disturbance. The owl took off from a nearby perch, wings flapping in raucous commotion. Lulu's gaze dropped down, and as though sensing a presence, she faced Bailey.

Their eyes met.

Lulu's mouth widened, and she gasped, no doubt astounded given Bailey's mud-saturated state. Bailey imagined she appeared cartoonish, a monstrous swamp creature arisen from the bowels of the earth. The moment of shock was the one break Bailey had been praying for. She spotted the revolver lying only inches from Lulu's right hand, and then she lunged at the kneeling woman, throwing all her weight against her solid bulk.

The back of Lulu's head hit the tree—hard, with a dull thump that Bailey hoped would knock her out cold. But she only grunted before clamping her strong hands on Bailey's arms and squeezing with enough force that Bailey cried out in pain. Lulu might be thirty years her senior, but she was as strong as hate mixed with vinegar.

Bailey kneed her in the stomach and managed

to kick the revolver several feet away. The grip on her arms loosened and Lulu groaned.

"Stop," she pleaded. "Please."

Bailey backed off, breathing heavily as Lulu gasped for breath and struggled to her knees.

"How could you?" Bailey asked in a thin voice. "How could you be with a killer? He's a monster."

Lulu's eyes gleamed with fury at the insult to Holt. "Don't you dare judge me."

Bailey stared, mesmerized. This woman was a stranger, one she'd never truly known until this moment. Hard to believe that she was the same person who'd fixed her dinners and chatted as they kept each other company many a long evening.

Lulu gathered her energy and made a sudden leap at the pistol gleaming in the moonlight.

That was what Bailey got for showing a moment of weakness. Mercy repaid by yet another attempt.

Bailey jumped on top of the woman and pinned her arm back. Lulu bucked and twisted beneath her like a wild animal—spitting and hissing. They rolled on the ground, kicking and punching. Lulu had difficulty maintaining a grasp on her mud-slimed body. The woman's hands slipped and fell away at every attempt to gain purchase.

At least Bailey had that going for her. With every roll, Bailey's eyes sought the gun; it was her focal point in the mad moonlit dance. If she could just reach it…

She slid from Lulu's grasp and inched her body to the right, her fingers hitting the gun's cold metal barrel. Another inch…there, she had it. Her fingers curled around the barrel and she slid it closer to her body. But she needed to distract Lulu before raising the weapon.

"It's Holt," she croaked, affixing her gaze just past Lulu's left shoulder.

Lulu's eyes narrowed with suspicion, but she looked back over her shoulder into the gaping darkness.

There would be no mercy this time. Bailey swung the pistol as hard as she could, making contact with Lulu's right temple. With a thud, the woman's stout torso crumbled and fell upon her. Bailey quickly rolled away from the dead weight and stood over Lulu, holding the gun and aiming it at her with steady hands.

Lulu lay motionless.

"Playing possum?" Bailey asked. Her voice was hard and gravelly, unrecognizable even to herself. She slowly inched to Lulu's side, never lowering the gun. A stream of blood ran in rivulets down the right side of the woman's face.

Tentatively, she kicked at her hip, rolling

Lulu onto her back. Still no movement from the prone, inert body. Bailey couldn't bring herself to believe she was out for good. She laid a wet sneaker on Lulu's stomach, gradually shifting the full weight of her body in her gut. When Lulu didn't move, Bailey nodded in satisfaction. No one could fake it that well.

She stepped away from the body and tucked the gun in the waistband of her shorts. Might come in handy before the night was over. If Lulu or Holt caught up to her, she'd have no hesitation shooting to kill.

Bailey tugged the leather cord off her neck and flung the crow feather necklace at the motionless Lulu. "Keep your talismans."

She glanced around, formulating a new course of action. If Edgar were a halfway decent human being, she could arrive at his house in fifteen minutes and ask him to phone the police. The next neighbor was another mile or two down the road, but that was her best option. She'd rather opt for the kindness of strangers than Edgar.

Which meant she had a long walk in front of her. Bailey moved her exhausted, wooden legs forward. The main road was up past the barn. She'd stay to the forest alongside the road, keeping cover in case Holt drove along searching for her. Decision made, she cast one last look at Lulu and then shoved off. When all this was over, she'd soak at least an hour in a hot bath and then sleep like a baby. The thought of warm water caressing her skin gave Bailey strength. She could even smell the clean scent of soap and shampoo as it washed away every last trace of mud and slime.

Vines, thorns and palmetto leaves shredded her legs and arms, while mosquitoes nipped everywhere. But Bailey kept plodding along, even when she wanted nothing more than to curl into a ball and bed down in pine needles like a fawn.

Maybe just one little rest. A few moments to recoup her energy. She leaned against a cypress and sagged into its support.

From afar, a pack of dogs howled and barked. Instantly she stiffened, alert as a hunted animal. Edgar's dogs. She whirled in a circle, trying to determine from what direction they were coming. Hadn't Dylan told Edgar to keep them contained? They clearly were not. Her skin crawled as she remembered the last attack when she was a teenager, the terror as the alpha had bitten her, his canine teeth sinking into her hip and remaining there, burning like hot metal spikes, while the others circled her body, growling and snapping their bared fangs. She'd expected a savage death, her flesh shredded to a bloody pulp. But the other dogs hadn't joined in as they awaited Edgar's command when he'd found her.

You have a gun this time. Use it.

She didn't even know how many bullets were loaded. Would it be enough? By the time the dogs were close enough for her to shoot, it might well be too late.

She needed higher ground. Bailey eyed the trees, seeking one suitable for climbing. All the while, the Dobermans howled in a frenzy of bloodlust. They were closer now. Desperately she located a live oak with low-lying branches and began to climb.

The first dog rounded the copse of trees, black fur blending into the night and accenting his white fangs. Others followed, and within seconds the whole gang had arrived. Did they remember her? Bailey desperately grasped the next branch, pulling her body up in small spurts. Another branch, another foot upward to safety.

But she wasn't fast enough. Teeth bore into her right ankle. She screamed and tried to kick at the dog with her other foot, but he was impervious to her attempts, only seeming to dig his fangs in further, tugging her body down. She hung from a branch, flailing in panic.

"Edgar! Stop them." Was he even with his animals? Usually he was, awake at the first bark of trouble.

Her palms were slick with sweat as she tried not to lose her grip. There was no way to fish the gun from her waistband and maintain her hold on the limb with her free hand. Her arms reached the breaking point and lost the tug-of-war battle. The fall was short, but the dogs were on her in an instant. The growls were everywhere, so menacing and close she felt their vibration seep into her flesh, shaking her to the core.

For the second time in her life, she lay trapped as they kept her pinned to the ground. Hot saliva slobbered her neck, fangs grazing her throat. One wrong move, and that steel jaw would tighten, crushing her airway.

She was trapped.

Chapter Sixteen

The streets were deserted as Dylan slipped the key into the warehouse lock. Since he was too wound up to sleep, he might as well investigate the small matter that niggled at the back of his mind.

Sure enough, Janet Blackwell and her lover had been found at a motel in Atlanta, running away to start a new life by ditching their spouses. Would have saved law enforcement time and money if they'd bothered to tell someone their plans. At least that was one less matter to distract them from their search for a serial killer. And it also left him free to check old police records.

His father would never have ignored a child being mistreated, and Dylan meant to prove it—to himself as much as Bailey. He eyed the stacks of cardboard boxes as he stepped into the warehouse and sighed. Jeff had done him a huge favor today and checked the microfilm documents. None of his father's old case notes had locking up. The streets remained deserted and he drove slowly, feeling restless. He double-checked his phone—still no word from Bailey. She must be asleep. Apparently, everyone in Folkston was sleeping but him.

He'd swing by where she was staying. A quick drive-by to make sure all was in order. All he cared about was her safety. Once he'd determined nothing looked amiss, he'd finally be able to sleep. Dylan met his rueful smile in the car's dashboard mirror. *Oh, heck*. Bailey had totally captured his heart.

Chapter Seventeen

Dog stink permeated her nose and lungs with every shallow breath. It even seemed to seep into her very pores. Bailey imagined the scent would remain with her forever—that is, if she made it through the night. Had she escaped Lulu and evaded Holt only to land right back in her worst childhood nightmare? She cursed fate, willing her anger to override the terror.

Did she even want Edgar to find her this time? If nothing else, having the dogs around her would dissuade Holt from snatching her up. If Edgar didn't come, she could lie here the rest of the night until Dylan realized she was in trouble and a search team was called out.

But that was hours and hours away. The thought of breathing in the dogs' hot, panting breaths and listening to their growls for that length of time consumed her with a familiar panic. She'd rather face an armed Holt than this. Anything but this.

Pinned in by the dogs, on the ground, she kept her eyes scrunched closed to avoid the sight of their snipping fangs and their glaring eyes. If she was to be eaten alive, she'd rather not see the gruesome bloodbath. The gun was cold and hard against her hip, but if she moved to get it, the dogs might go into a frenzy. Too risky.

The unmistakable click of a bullet being pumped into a shotgun chamber rang out. Her eyes popped open. The crunch of footsteps approached.

"Who's out there?" a gruff voice called out. "You're on my property."

Edgar. She'd recognize that voice anywhere. Bailey didn't answer, afraid the dogs' taut eagerness to attack would tip over the edge if she made any noise. Her throat closed so tightly that Bailey wasn't even sure she was capable of speech.

He was near her now. The ground vibrated with the weight of his steps. The dogs peered up at their master, awaiting his command. His shadow loomed over her body, blocking the moonlight. Edgar blinked down at her, shotgun aimed at her chest, then chuckled.

"That you, Bailey? Damn. You been crawling around in a mud pond? You don't look good."

Her throat worked, but no sound emerged.

"Cat got your tongue?" he asked. "Never thought to find you pinned down like this again."

He leaned the shotgun barrel against his shoulder, now that he realized the intruder was no threat to him. "No, sir. Not since the last time you ran from me."

Bailey found her voice. "Call. Them. Off."

"Why should I? What you doin' on my land? Spying on me?"

"I've got better things to do."

He tilted his head back and laughed. "Think you're some big shot now, coming around here and telling tales on me to that cop you were with. Didn't do you no good last time when you tried it, and it won't do you no good now."

She challenged him. "You sure about that?"

A flicker of unease crossed his face. "You threatening me?"

"Call off your dogs and we'll talk."

Edgar rubbed the back of his neck and scowled, evidently weighing the pros and cons of having the Dobermans feast on her flesh. At last, he pointed at the dogs and growled, "Get back, ya hear?"

They whined in protest, but Edgar lifted a leg as if to soccer kick them into kingdom come, and they begrudgingly complied. Instantly Bailey scrambled to her feet, wincing as her right ankle bore her weight. "One of them bit me," she spat out.

"You were trespassin'. You're lucky they didn't tear you to pieces."

Bailey gritted her teeth together to keep him from seeing her tremble. She had to deal with Edgar from a position of strength and not let him believe he had total control.

"And what if they did kill me? You think you'd get away with murder after a cop warned you to keep them locked up?"

His chin rose and his eyes almost squinted shut. All signs he was very close to losing his temper. "Why are you here?"

There was no reason to lie. "I found out your neighbor, Holt Rucker, is a killer. I'm on the run from him."

"Holt? A killer?" Edgar's voice rose to a squeak. "You're joking, right?"

"Do you see me laughing? He's somewhere out here looking for me. Thanks to all the yapping of your stupid dogs, he might be really close."

"Holt? You out there?" Edgar called out in a singsong voice, mocking her explanation. "Olly olly oxen free!"

"Shut up!"

His face hardened. "Get off my land and stay off." He gestured to the dogs. "Let's get on home, boys."

Edgar turned his back on her and walked

away. She blinked in surprise at his sudden departure. "Wait!"

He kept walking.

Bailey limped along after him. "Stop! You can't just leave me alone out here. I need your help."

"Ain't no law says I got to help you," he called over his shoulder, picking up his pace to a brisk trot, the Dobermans racing in front of him, eager to be home.

She struggled to walk with her injured right ankle. "But...but..."

On he walked. It was useless. The man had no mercy in him. Never did and never would. She was on her own.

Anger roiled through her body. She grasped the gun's handle and pulled it out of her waistband, then raised her arm and pointed at the man who'd caused her so much grief. Revenge was only a click away.

Her finger trembled on the trigger.

Edgar disappeared into the dark and the anger left her as swiftly as it had flared. She lowered her arm and shook at what she'd even dared contemplate.

Bailey hugged her muddy arms to her chest and glanced around, certain that Holt was nearby, ready to grab her and force her into a black oblivion. She'd be like Mary and Amy and Lisa and who knew how many others, never to be seen or heard from again.

Keep walking. Get to the road and keep the gun at your side, that calm, inner voice advised. She inhaled deeply to get her bearings and determine which direction to go. Best to follow the narrow trail toward Edgar's and then veer to the left at the next clearing. Bailey set off, hoping she was heading in the right direction. The pain in her ankle slowed her down, but she kept going forward.

Only minutes into the journey, the back of her neck suddenly prickled, and she whirled around. A large column of black stood only six feet behind her. The figure moved, breaking up the pattern. She discerned a length of the darkness breaking away and rising upward.

An arm.

Holding a gun.

Pointed at her.

"Drop your weapon!" he shouted.

She did. No way to use it before he could fire a round at her first.

Bailey's mouth went dry and she instinctively stretched out her arms, throwing her hands in front of her face. As if that would ward off a bullet.

The column moved toward her until Holt's gaunt face appeared, the pale blue eyes as piercing as the night they'd materialized mere inches from her face in the homestead window. The sort of gleam that only the truly insane sported. A potpourri of paranoia, rage and a coldness that resulted from a total lack of human warmth.

Pleading for mercy would be pointless. As would running. She could only hope to appeal to whatever remained of his rational mind.

"Don't shoot me, Holt. There's a witness nearby."

Holt stepped closer, his gun still pointed at her torso. "Slacomb? He's gone. I heard you pleading with him. You'll get no help from that quarter."

Never removing his eyes from her, he used his foot to slide her weapon closer to him. "Never cared for the man or his dogs, but tonight all the commotion made you easy to find. I owe him one."

Those two should get along famously, she thought. Both cold, vicious and with no regard for life.

"Why?" she whispered. "Why are you doing this? What have you done to the others?"

"Never mind that." His voice was hard and his motions fast as bullets as he picked up the gun and tucked it in his waistband. "What'd you do to Lulu?"

She didn't want to add fuel to his temper's fire.

"Nothing," she lied. "I gave her the slip. Not that it did me any good."

He was on her in a flash, grabbing a fistful of her hair and sticking the gun's nozzle into her burning scalp. "No games. Where is she?"

"At least…" she hissed in oxygen through the searing pain "…a mile back. I—I can show you." Tears streamed down her face, and although she knew it was pointless, she added, "Please."

The grip loosened, but Holt's eyes were no less menacing. "If you've hurt her—"

"No. No. I couldn't hurt a friend." Lies were easy when they bought you precious time to live, and to plan your next move to keep on living.

"Where?" he demanded.

"I'll show you." There. She could spend hours leading him on a wild-goose chase. Would it be enough time? How much longer until morning broke and Dylan tried to contact her?

"Just tell me."

"It's not far from the barn. I can't say exactly."

"Get moving, then."

His hand circled her upper arm, bruising and merciless. "Don't try and run away," he warned. "I'll find you. No matter what. I'll always find you." He let go and pushed her forward. Light exploded, illuminating the path ahead. With one hand he held the flashlight, and with the other, he kept the gun digging into her lower spine. "Go," he ordered.

Bailey obeyed, her mind racing as each step brought her closer to the barn. Should she claim to be lost? Or should she eventually take him to Lulu? When Holt spotted her body, perhaps he'd be distracted by grief and she could grab one of the guns or run away.

"How'd you get away from her?" Holt asked as they pressed ever forward.

"I'm decades younger. I have better eyesight and can outrun her."

"Liar. How'd you get her gun, then?"

He had her there. The beam of light wavered in front of her as he drew his arm back and lifted it as though to strike.

"Okay, okay. I'll tell you the truth."

Holt lowered his hand. "Keep walking and talking."

"I realized she'd slipped something in my drink. I went to the back bedroom and heard her on the phone with you." Even now the horror of that moment knifed her gut. "I opened the window and ran away. She followed me."

She tripped on a root and lost her footing. Holt grabbed her hair again and pulled her up. She couldn't stop the scream of pain. He loosened his hold. "Go on. Walk and talk. Remember?"

"Th-then she caught up with me. We got in a

tussle. I wrestled the gun from her and hit her in the head with it. I don't know how badly she's hurt." No need to mention that she'd left Lulu unconscious. "Then I just ran."

"You better not have shot her," Holt rasped. "If you did, you'll suffer extra."

Had Lulu survived the blow to the head? Her only hope might be that the head injury had slammed some sense into her former friend's mind. That Lulu would magically return to the person Bailey once thought she was.

But there was no magic. Only this slow, steady midnight progression toward the barn and certain death.

By the thin glow of the flashlight came the outline of the old barn. Bailey's legs felt heavy at the sight and she abruptly halted.

"Get moving," he said. The guttural command screamed near her ears. It ricocheted inside her mind like bullets.

"No. If you're going to kill me, do it now." She'd rather get a quick bullet than whatever torture Holt had in mind.

Her knees trembled, and she gulped in humid air that was sticky and heavy and cloying. She prayed Dylan wouldn't be the person who found her body. Bailey sank to her knees and stared at the full moon, wondering how many seconds she had left to live. She thought of Dylan and the tender way he kissed her, the way he had moaned in her arms the night they'd spent together.

And now it was all over. One night—no more chances to repeat that magic. But she had no regrets, only a deep thankfulness he'd come into her life, no matter if it was only to be for a short time. Because at last, she knew what it meant to love a man. To utterly and completely trust him and want to be with him the rest of her life.

"Get up. You ain't getting off so easy." Holt kicked the middle of her back with his heavy boot and she fell onto her face. Her teeth cut into her upper lip and she tasted blood mixed with mud.

"You've caused me too much trouble already."

Bailey rose to her feet and kept walking. What did it matter if he beat her to death here or in the barn? Both choices ended with the same result.

"Why have you hurt so many people?" she asked, trying to make sense of what was happening to her and what had befallen the other victims.

"Because I can."

It was as simple and awful as that.

Bailey plunged into the barn and the darkness deepened. Only a few slats of moonbeams shone through openings in the rotting wood. Holt jerked her by the arm, pulling her next to a rusted farm machine that looked like it hadn't been used for at least a decade.

"Don't move," he warned.

The flashlight fell to the ground, and from his back pants pocket he pulled out two small orbs of silver that glistened.

Handcuffs, she realized with horror. *Heck, no. Run!*

Bailey twisted to the side and tried to skirt around Holt. He grabbed her forearms and pushed her against the rusted metal. This was her only chance. Once he got those cuffs on her, she was a dead woman.

She kicked at his shins and groin, fighting as wild and desperate as a cornered animal. One blow landed and Holt groaned and bent over double, placing his hands on his thighs. She darted past him and ran for the door. Freedom was only a foot away when Holt tackled her from behind and she fell face-first.

A scream echoed in the barn. Had that been her?

Hands clamped over her injured right ankle and dragged her back to the tractor. Bailey squirmed and kicked, landing a few blows to his legs. Holt didn't even seem to notice, as though she were as harmless as a gnat.

"No!" She screamed until her throat was raw. But who was out there to hear her cry for help?

Edgar? He wouldn't lift a finger to save her. He'd already made that clear.

She continued kicking and screaming—even after she heard the metal gears of the cuff grind around one wrist. Metal slammed against metal—a death knell. The fight drained from her.

Holt's lips twisted into a mockery of a smile. "Scream all you want. It'll do no good." He cocked his head toward the back corner of the barn. "Just ask Amy."

Amy? Bailey whipped her head around, seeking the other woman. "She's alive? In here?"

"Barely."

Holt's fingers dug in her chin and he forced her head around. Those crazy blue eyes were only inches from her face. "I'm going to find Lulu. And she better not be dead, or you'll pay dearly."

He picked the flashlight up off the floor and flicked its beam to the back corner. "Say hello to your new neighbor, Amy."

Bailey inhaled sharply when the light pinpointed a woman whose hands and feet were bound with rope. A number of bruises and patches of dried blood were scattered over her naked body.

Amy Holley didn't so much as whimper.

Holt laughed, the sight of her suffering seeming to lift his dour spirits. "See you ladies in a bit."

The minute he faded from sight, Bailey breathed a tiny bit easier. She tugged at the cuffs, which didn't loosen an inch.

Her mind flooded with a darkness that matched the night. This wasn't her first time being bound. Not by a long shot. It had been Edgar's favorite means to discipline her, to break her spirit and bend her to his will. Somehow she'd found the strength to escape him, refusing to become a shadow of woman like his wife, Millie.

Don't panic. Don't accept this fate.

Bailey fought through the panic and despair. "Amy?" she called out. "Everyone's been looking for you. How badly are you hurt?"

"I wish I was dead."

The sound of Amy's voice, so flat and void of hope, pinched Bailey's heart. She had to find a way to get them out of this prison. Amy needed her.

"We're going to get out of here," she assured Amy. "I promise."

Bailey forced her breathing back to normal and searched rationally for ideas. She'd seen plenty of internet videos recently on how to escape zip-tie bindings, but these were actual cuffs.

Holt had used a tiny key to lock the cuffs. Stood to reason that if she had a sharp piece of metal, she could jimmy the lock. But where? With her free hand, she patted down her pockets, nothing there, then glanced at her muddy sneakers. Nothing there, either. She wore no barrettes and had never bothered with bobby pins, not even when her hair was long enough for a ponytail.

She swallowed down a lump of fear. She carried nothing of use, which meant she had to find a piece of metal, or a sliver of something sharp nearby. Her eyes cast around the barn littered with abandoned farm equipment. But all the machinery within her reach was big and clunky—entirely useless for lock picking. She glided one foot, and then another, covering the ground in a semicircle—like a trapped ballerina.

Her shins connected with something solid. Something long and wooden. A hollowed trough, she realized. There were several rows of them. This place must have once been a pig farm. She groaned, kicking the trough until the bottoms of her feet blistered. The rotten wood easily cracked and splintered, the shards nesting by her feet. Though long and sharp, they were entirely too fragile for her purpose.

She swiped at them with the sides of her feet, cursing under her breath, willing the anger to provide strength. Anything was preferable to despair. The shards scattered, and in the remaining debris something glittered. She peered closely until recognition dawned.

It was a nail. A long, thin nail.

"Yes!" She raised her free fist and pumped the stale, humid air. "Amy, we're in luck."

Amy whimpered. Bailey twisted to face her, but could only see her pale, naked body hunkered into a tight ball. The woman must be so traumatized that hope had long since fled.

"Hang in there, Amy," she said softly.

Bailey returned her focus to the nail, even more determined to shed her handcuffs. Time was ticking away at an alarming rate. She stretched a leg, pointed her toes and reached for the nail. It brushed the tip of her sneakers—just out of reach. Bailey leaned forward another inch, crying out as the cuffs cut into her wrist. And she was still too short to pull it into reach.

There had to be a way.

Bailey kicked off her sneakers and grasped one of the broken wood pieces between her toes. Carefully, she again strained forward and brushed the nail toward her with her improvised, primitive tool. It took several attempts, but she managed to grasp the nail between her toes and lift it to her free hand.

She wanted to weep with victory. Still, the hardest part was yet to come. She had zero experience picking a lock, but survival was a powerful motivator. Fumbling, she inserted the rusted point of the nail into the keyhole and wiggled it. Nothing.

"Come on, come on," she muttered, trying it over and over.

A click pinged in the still darkness. The lock mechanism surrendered its hold.

"It worked!" she shouted, tears of joy and relief wetting her face. She flung the handcuffs away. They thudded against a wall and dropped out of sight. Quickly she slipped back on her sneakers and ran to the back of the barn.

Amy's shoulders rose all the way to her ears, and she lifted both bound hands in front of her face.

Bailey slowed to a walk, holding out her hand. "It's okay, Amy," she said gently. "I'm not going to hurt you."

She crouched in front of the huddled woman, wanting to reassure her and not make any sudden moves, while at the same time looking over her shoulder, expecting Holt to return at any moment.

"Let's get out of this place." She touched Amy's hands, gently lowering them from her face. "First I'll untie you, okay?"

At Amy's reluctant nod, Bailey set to work. The rope binding was tight, but she soon had it loosened. Amy gasped and moaned as the rope slid against her abrasions. "Sorry, hon. Stretch out your feet now," Bailey instructed. "We're almost there."

Amy untucked her legs and Bailey pulled at the binding, keeping eyes and ears on alert for Holt. At last she had the ropes off.

"Can you stand?" she asked.

Amy bit her lip and nodded. She rose halfway up on her legs, wobbly as a newborn fawn.

Bailey slipped an arm under Amy's shoulders. "Lean against me. I've got you. Let's walk now and get the heck away."

Amy's eyes filled with tears and something new—hope. "Thank you," she said simply.

Slowly they made their way to the barn door. Bailey strove for patience, but despite her outward calm and optimism for Amy, her stomach churned, and her mind screamed for her to run as fast as possible from the danger.

At the door, Bailey peered out, checking to see if the coast was clear. She didn't see anyone, but she was sure that Holt had a hidden camera mounted nearby, just as he had at the old church where he'd temporarily kept his victims. The killer closely monitored his makeshift prisons in case of an escape or an intruder, always managing to keep a step ahead of being discovered.

"We're good, but we need to hurry," she said, pulling Amy out and urging her to move faster. Between her injured ankle and Amy's overall weakness, progress was slow. Somehow, they had to make it to the road and flag down the first driver for help.

She breathed a little easier once they made it out of the clearing and into the cover of trees—but they were never going to make it to the road in time to be saved. Not at this pace.

What to do? She couldn't just abandon Amy to be caught yet again by Holt. Or, just as bad, attacked by Edgar's dogs.

You have to save yourself first to save Amy.

Bailey drew to a stop. "It's at least another two miles to the road. I'm going to have to make a run for it."

Amy stared at her with huge eyes, and the slight glimmer of hope that had flared in them died. Her fingers dug into Bailey's arm. "Don't leave me," she begged. "He'll find me. Please!"

"I'll come back for you. I promise." Bailey disengaged from Amy's grasp. "I'll find you a hiding place and then I'll come back with the cops. This is our best chance. You're going to be okay, Amy. Just hold out a little longer."

Bailey scanned the area, spotting an oak that would do. She tugged on Amy's arm, urging her toward the tree. "I don't want to scare you even more, but there's a pack of vicious dogs roaming out here. You'll be safer up in a tree."

"Dogs?" She fearfully glanced around.

Bailey pointed at the tree. "They won't hurt you up there."

It took more persuading and strength she didn't know she had in reserve before Bailey, using a combination of her pulling and Amy climbing as best she could, got Amy safely ensconced in the uppermost branches of the tree.

"I'll be back soon. Shh," she whispered, placing a finger in front of her pursed lips.

Amy nodded and laid her head to rest on a limb, arms and legs bracketing its thickness.

Bailey scrambled down the tree and hit the ground running—as fast as she could with an injured ankle. Trees and thick underbrush loomed, preventing a quick escape. Finally, what seemed like hours later, she saw lights flicker from the road, strobing through the woods a few seconds before disappearing. Headlights. Relief whooshed through her lungs. She was so very close now.

Twigs snapped, and leaves rustled from behind. *Not now! Please. Not when I'm almost home free. Not with Amy depending on me for her life.* Bailey upped her speed, her heart jackhammering against her ribs.

Just a little farther to go.

Chapter Eighteen

A truck slowly approached, blinding Dylan with bright headlight beams. What was it doing on this lonesome road way past midnight? Judging from the truck's überslow speed, he guessed the person was returning home from a night of drinking at a bar, inebriated and driving at a snail's pace to keep from running off the road. Dylan frowned, wishing he were in his cop car so he could pull the driver over.

"Your destination is on the right," came the disembodied voice of the GPS.

Dylan pushed down on his brake, easing his car to the side of the road. Bailey's car was in the driveway as well as a light blue sedan he recognized as belonging to her neighbor, Lulu. The tidy home was dark, and he had no reason to doubt both women were ensconced inside, sound asleep and in no danger.

The other truck rambled alongside him and he caught a fleeting glimpse of a gray-haired man staring out his window, his eyes piercing and glaring at him with suspicion, before he picked up speed and passed. Why that look? Dylan shrugged it off as he continued down the road. Maybe the fellow lived nearby and thought Dylan was the suspicious-looking one by pulling off the street and staring at his neighbor's house.

There was no cause for alarm, yet he shifted uneasily in his seat. Bailey might be annoyed but he wouldn't rest easy until he heard her voice. He picked up his cell phone and called her.

It rang five times before switching to voice mail. He flung the phone on the empty seat beside him. Ridiculous or not, he had to know she was okay. He grabbed the steering wheel and started to make a U-turn when a movement from the woods caught his eye.

A mud-covered figure stumbled from the tree line, waving its arms and limping toward his vehicle. Dylan strained his eyes to see into the darkness, then doubted the image he thought appeared before him. He was sleep-deprived and worried about Bailey, a volatile cocktail of emotions that caused his eyes to play tricks on him.

But no, he wasn't seeing things. The person drifted closer and he got a good luck at their face. Beneath the filth and blood crusting the mouth and chin, he'd recognize her no matter what.

"Bailey!" Dylan jumped out of the car. "What the heck—"

She threw herself onto him, and he felt her entire body trembling against his. A deep relief welled inside him. She was alive and here in his arms.

"We've got to get in the car," she said before he could question her. She withdrew from his arms and cast a fearful glance over her shoulder. "Holt's behind me."

"Holt Rucker? What's he got—"

"He's the killer," she said, limping to the passenger side and opening the door. "You've got to radio for backup. Amy's still back there."

For a moment, he stood rooted on the blacktop, his thoughts spinning and disjointed. A killer had been chasing Bailey through the woods, Amy was alive, Bailey was hurt and they were in danger.

Dylan sprinted back to his vehicle and called the emergency dispatcher, quickly explaining the situation and his location and requesting helicopter assistance. With their thermal imaging detectors, a chopper had the best chance of pinpointing Holt and Amy's whereabouts. He wanted to end this as quickly as possible and get Amy to safety. A sudden thought occurred. "What about your friend, Lulu? Is she also out there in the woods?"

A headlight pierced the darkness behind them. Dylan turned and narrowed his eyes, adjusting to the light's glare. It was the vehicle he'd spotted earlier. "Does Holt Rucker drive a blue truck?"

Bailey whipped her head around. "Yes. Is that him behind us?"

"That or someone's borrowed his vehicle. Buckle up and keep your head down below the window," he ordered, jerking the car around 180 degrees. He withdrew his gun and released the safety.

He was almost upon the truck when the driver rolled down his window. The long barrel of a shotgun extended, aimed smack dab at Dylan. He crouched below the dashboard, placing a hand on Bailey's shoulder to make sure she stayed down.

A second later, pellets exploded through the front windshield and shards of glass rained down on them.

Their vehicles were almost side by side now. Dylan rose up and shot at the driver. Damn it, he missed. Another shotgun blast and pain exploded in his left shoulder. He felt himself sinking, his world going to black. Only one thought formed in his quickly hazing mind. Bailey had gone through unspeakable trauma tonight, had outwitted Holt in the woods and made it to the road, only to have Dylan gunned down and be recaptured again—all when he was supposed to save her.

"Dylan!" He could tell she was screaming by the frantic edge to her voice—but it sounded as though she were far, far away. Strong hands shoved him to the passenger side, and her body slid over his and then took his place behind the wheel. His car lurched forward, and they were hurtling away into the darkness. He swallowed down the pain, took off his shirt and pressed it against the bloody wound. It hurt, but the pain braced him, and he sat up straight. Lucky for him, the damage was on his left shoulder instead of his right.

Bailey had taken command of the car, her foot bearing down hard on the accelerator. Through the side mirror he saw Holt still in pursuit and closing in. A roar sounded in the sky, lasting too long to be thunder. A blinding beam speared downward.

A rescue helicopter had arrived.

Police sirens also closed in from both directions, their blue lights flashing. The cop car behind Holt was rapidly gaining on him.

"Looks like he's the one trapped now," Bailey said with satisfaction as the blue truck screeched to a stop.

To his left was the great Okefenokee swamp, teeming with alligators, and to his right the woods.

The truck made a sudden lurch to the right.

"He's going to make a run through the woods. Let me drive."

Bailey shook her head, sharply turning his vehicle around and taking it off-road. "I've got this." They bounced along the sandy soil, other cops following their lead. The helicopter hovered overhead, clearly spotlighting Holt as he exited his truck, still carrying the shotgun.

He grabbed Bailey's arm as she opened her door. "You're not going out there."

"But—"

"No way."

Other officers got out of their vehicles. They commanded Holt to surrender and finally, realizing there was no escape, he threw down his weapon. Cops swarmed him.

"It's over now," he reassured Bailey. "We've got the guy. Thanks to you."

"But Amy's still out there. I have to show you where she's hidden."

"The helicopters will spot her."

"You don't understand. She's traumatized. I want to be there when she's found. I told her I'd return, and she trusts me."

Dylan nodded. All he wanted was to take Bailey home and keep her safe, to comfort her after the trauma of the night. To feel her heartbeat thumping against him. But he understood her need to help Amy. "Okay, but we go together."

They got out of his vehicle and found Sheriff Chesser, quickly explaining the situation and roughly where to direct the helicopters to find Amy. He nodded his assent, insisting that backup escort them to the site.

It didn't take them long to spot Amy. The helicopters had arrived first, and their lights flashed down on an emaciated woman who cowered in the treetop, clinging to a limb as though drowning in the storm of sudden light, wind and sound.

"Amy!" Bailey jumped up and down, waving her arms, but Amy's gaze was locked on the helicopter above, and Dylan doubted the woman could hear Bailey over the chopper motor.

Bailey started up the tree and he followed, hoping Amy would allow him to carry her down to safety. The wound on his left shoulder throbbed, but not enough to incapacitate him. Ambulances with EMTs were on standby in the clearing, waiting to take her to a hospital.

Bailey reached her first and leaned over Amy, cautiously touching her shoulder. The woman recoiled with a scream.

"Amy, it's me, Bailey. Remember? I told you I'd be back."

Amy's wide eyes flickered with terror before understanding dawned. She nodded, and Bailey took her hand, giving it a squeeze. "Time to come down now."

With great care, Amy sat up and then froze when she saw Dylan.

"This is my friend, Dylan," Bailey explained. "He's going to help you down if you need it."

Amy held out her hand to him and he clasped it, relieved she'd so easily accepted his presence. "I'll carry you. It'll be easier," he shouted over the chopper noise.

Bailey sidled out of his way and he scooped Amy in his arms, wincing at the throb in his left shoulder as he shifted her body weight onto his good arm. He marveled that an adult could weigh so little. Skeletal bones poked close to the surface of her skin.

When they reached the ground, Sheriff Chesser was already there, concern suffusing his face. He quickly wrapped a blanket around Amy. "I'll radio EMS to bring a stretcher out here. How's she doing?" He leaned in closer. "Ma'am, we're taking you to a hospital. We'll get a statement from you after you've been admitted and treated."

Amy ignored him and searched around frantically. "Bailey?"

She stepped closer to them. "I'm here."

Amy grasped her hand. "Stay with me."

"I'll stay by your side as long as you need me," Bailey reassured her.

Dylan's heart pinched at the exchange. It was only thanks to Bailey that this woman was still alive. Bailey was incredible—smart, compassionate and beautiful. A woman you'd be honored to have on your side in any situation.

And to think he'd come so close to losing her. Holt could easily have killed her tonight. A shudder ran down his back at the very thought of never seeing Bailey again, never having a chance to tell her how he felt, how he wanted her to be a part of his future.

He cleared his throat. "EMTs are taking too long. I'll carry Amy to the clearing."

Chesser spoke beside him. "Bailey—Dylan— you both need to have your injuries checked out, too."

The helicopter followed them, providing light as bright as an afternoon sun as they made their way slowly through the brush. How had Bailey navigated out here in the darkness with a killer on her heels? He was sure he'd have nightmares about this the rest of his life.

They burst into the clearing, by now awash with blue and red lights from over a dozen cop cars and ambulances. He rushed to the nearest ambulance, where an EMT met him and took over. Amy appeared bewildered at all the commotion and kept a tight grip on Bailey's hand.

"Don't leave me," she again pleaded with Bailey as they loaded the stretcher on the ambulance.

"I'm staying with you."

Bailey glanced up at him. "Are you coming with us? Your shoulder needs to be examined."

"I'll catch a ride with Chesser." The fewer people and less noise around Amy, the less her emotional distress.

"See you at the hospital later?" she asked.

He nodded, and the tightness in his throat spread to his chest. He had to tell Bailey how he felt about her. Now.

"Bailey, I—I…" His throat closed, and the words clogged deep inside.

Her eyes grew tender and a soft smile tugged the edges of her lips. "I know you care about me."

He found his voice and grasped her hand. "Care about you? That doesn't begin to express it. When I thought Holt might have killed you, my heart almost stopped beating. I was afraid I'd never get a chance to tell you that…" he swallowed hard past the lump in his throat "…that I'm in love with you, Bailey Covington. Day one, I was intrigued the moment you glared at me when I pulled you over on the ATV."

Her eyes misted as she softly chuckled. "I can't say I felt the same when you pulled me over, but through all this, I finally realized I could trust you with my life and my heart. I love you, too, Dylan."

An EMT interrupted with a stern command, "Time to go." Reluctantly, he released Bailey's hand. The EMT ushered him out, shutting the door of the ambulance. He watched as it sped out of the clearing, feeling like it was driving off with all the light and warmth of his world.

An arm clamped around his uninjured shoulder. "Ranger Covington's an amazing woman," Sheriff Chesser said. "She's going to be fine."

Epilogue

Pain exploded in her right thumb and Bailey dropped the hammer. "Damn it," she growled, shaking out her hand. This wasn't even her first mishap today.

Ace climbed into her lap, trying to slather her face with his tongue.

Absently, she rubbed behind his ears as she surveyed the doghouse she was building. Something was amiss. It tilted to the side and there were gaps in the slats. She gazed down at the directions, wondering how she'd gone so wrong.

A car pulled into the driveway and she moaned. She'd been so wrapped up with this project that time had slipped away. She and Dylan had made plans to picnic with his sister, Janie, and her daughter this afternoon. To Bailey's surprise, she enjoyed these outings with his loud, boisterous family. She'd lived a solitary existence for way too many years.

Dylan approached from the side of her cabin and, as always, her heart did a funny little thump.

She'd quickly gotten over her aversion to the Armstrong name, especially when he explained that his father had really tried to help her when she'd reached out to him as a teenager. It was just rotten luck that the abuse hadn't been committed in his jurisdiction and that the neighboring cop had been friends with Edgar.

Ace barked a greeting and ran to Dylan as she scrambled to her feet. He picked up Ace and ambled her way, tilting his head as he surveyed her handiwork.

She held up a hand. "Don't say it. Things went horribly astray at some point in the construction."

"If you want me to—"

"Nope. I'll figure it out."

He shrugged. "Don't know why you're wasting time building a doghouse. Ace stays inside with you all the time. I'd say he's fully enjoying his retirement from police searches."

"I worry about him when I'm at work. A dog needs to enjoy sunshine and run free, not be cooped up inside. I'm thinking my next project is to fence the backyard and then—" She broke off at the amusement in his eyes.

"This rascal has got you hooked around his little paws," he said with a laugh. "I'm jealous."

She laughed with him. Dylan had no reason to be jealous, as he well knew. Ever since Holt's arrest six weeks ago, they'd been almost inseparable, spending practically every night together either at his place or her cabin.

Dylan set Ace on the ground and his expression turned serious.

"What's up?" she asked at once.

"I'm going by Edgar Slacomb's place."

Her good mood soured at the man's name. "Why?"

"I have a bone to pick with him. And something needs to be done about those dogs. They're a danger to the community."

"He refuses to keep them penned."

"Exactly. Anyway, it occurred to me you might want to come along. Confront him for leaving you alone and injured in the woods while you were being hunted." Dylan's voice shook with anger and his whole body grew tight.

"Easy," she cautioned. "Maybe Jeff or another officer should handle this. Someone with no emotional investment."

"No, I'm going," he insisted. "I need to do this."

She drew a deep breath. "I think I do, too."

"You sure?" His olive green eyes bore into her, alight with concern.

"Yes. Let's do it now, before Janie's picnic."

He nodded, and they walked to the front of her cabin. Ace ran ahead to Dylan's car, anticipating an outing.

"Oh, no, you don't, little fellow. Those Dobermans would make mincemeat of you." She scooped him up and left him in the cabin before rejoining Dylan. As usual, her gaze flickered to Lulu's empty cabin.

She hadn't killed her former friend that night. Lulu had suffered a concussion and had been treated, right before the police had arrested her for accessory to murder and locked her up in the Charlton County jail to await trial. Holt Rucker, deemed more of a security threat and escape risk, was waiting in a maximum-security facility.

The sight of Lulu's cabin churned her gut as she remembered the betrayal. It didn't make sense, and Bailey recognized it never would. Not even if she lived to be a hundred. She'd tried to look back; had there been signs she'd missed along the way?

But no. No, there were not. She had no idea her friend was so lonely and desperate she'd go along with murder to keep a boyfriend who was in and out of her life. Maybe Bailey had projected her own feelings onto Lulu, assuming her own contentment with solitude was the same for the older woman. That seemed so long ago. She'd never want to go back to a such a solitary existence. With Dylan by her side, life was much richer and enjoyable. Sharing time with him was her greatest happiness.

Bailey shook off the thoughts of Lulu and climbed into Dylan's car. He shot her an understanding sideways glance.

"Maybe you should think about moving," he suggested.

"Maybe one day. We'll see."

They sped down the familiar roads to the Slacomb house, but this time it barely bothered her. She'd survived that night, no thanks to him, and if she could get through that, she could handle anything.

Dylan pulled up to the house. The mechanic garage was closed and there were no signs of any dogs, but as they exited the vehicle and walked to the front door, the barking began, somewhere near the back of the house.

Bailey gripped the canister of mace in her hands. She'd made a concession that a few dogs, like Ace, were okay—but these Dobermans were an altogether different matter.

Dylan knocked on the door and Millie opened it.

"Where are the dogs?" Dylan asked at once.

"Got 'em penned 'round back. They can't hurt you."

"Penned?" Bailey blurted. She'd never imagined Edgar would agree to that.

"Yes. Want me to show you?"

"I'd like to confirm they're no longer a menace," Dylan said.

They trooped around back. Sure enough, a large area of the yard was now fenced in chain link. The Dobermans rushed the barricade, barking and snarling.

"How did you get Edgar to agree to this?" she asked Millie. "And where is he? I have a few things I'd like to say to him."

Millie faced her, and Bailey noticed a fading yellow bruise on her left eye. "He's gone. Been gone over a week now."

Dylan gave a satisfied nod. "Glad to see he's being sensible about those dogs. Tell him I'd like to speak with him when he gets back."

Dylan's phone rang, and he fished it out of his pocket. "Excuse me," he said, stepping away to take the call.

Bailey shifted awkwardly. "Are you okay?" she finally asked.

"Better than I've been in years."

Bailey regarded her closely. Something *was* different about Millie—a certain ease and quiet confidence she'd never seen with her former foster mother.

Millie wet her thin lips. "I'm sorry about… you know…everything in the past. I hope you can forgive me."

Bailey drew a deep breath, recalling the many times Millie had turned her head and done nothing to stop the abuse. She'd bet this woman had been a victim, too. "I'm willing to let it go," she said slowly. "Edgar's a different story, though."

"Don't worry about Edgar." A new conviction

rang in Millie's voice. "Neither of us will ever be seeing him again."

"We're both better off without him," Bailey said with a nod.

Their eyes locked another moment before Dylan returned, stuffing his phone in his pocket. "Ready to go?" he asked.

"Ready."

She turned on her heel and took his hand as they walked back to his car. *Ready.* She'd never been more ready to leave the past behind, especially now that he was in her life. As though sensing her feelings, Dylan brushed a quick kiss on her forehead. "You never have to come back to this place," he said.

"I don't plan on it." Impulsively, she wrapped her arms around his neck and kissed him.

He laughed and hugged her close. "What brought this on?"

"I'm just happy. Truly happy. Because of you."

Dylan cupped her chin in his hands. "I always want to make you feel this way. Always," he vowed, his voice husky.

Always. Yes, it was what she wanted as well. She kissed him—a long, long kiss full of promise and hope for their future. Together.

* * * * *

COMING NEXT MONTH FROM

◆ HARLEQUIN

INTRIGUE

Available May 19, 2020

#1929 AMBUSH BEFORE SUNRISE
Cardwell Ranch: Montana Legacy • by B.J. Daniels
Wrangler Angus Savage has come to Wyoming to reconnect with
Jinx McCallahan and help her get her cattle to high country. But when they
set out on the trail, they don't expect to come across so many hazards—
including Jinx's treacherous ex, who wants her back...or dead.

#1930 MIDNIGHT ABDUCTION
Tactical Crime Division • by Nichole Severn
When Benning Reeves's twins are kidnapped, the frantic father asks
Ana Ramirez and the Tactical Crime Division of the FBI for help. As evidence
accumulates, they'll have to discover why this situation connects to an
unresolved case...before it's too late.

#1931 EVASIVE ACTION
Holding the Line • by Carol Ericson
Minutes before her wedding, April Hart learns her fiancé is a drug lord. Now
the only person she can trust is a man from her past—border patrol agent
Clay Archer. April left Clay to protect him from her dangerous family, so this
time Clay is determined to guard April—and his heart.

#1932 WHAT SHE SAW
Rushing Creek Crime Spree • by Barb Han
Deputy Courtney Foster's brief fling with Texas ranch owner Jordan Kent
was her time-out after getting shot in the line of duty. Only now she's
hunting a killer...and she just discovered she's pregnant.

#1933 ISOLATED THREAT
A Badlands Cops Novel • by Nicole Helm
When Cecilia Mills asks sheriff's deputy Brady Wyatt to help her hide a child
from his father's biker gang, Brady will put his life on the line to keep all
three of them safe from the Sons of the Badlands.

#1934 WITHOUT A TRACE
An Echo Lake Novel • by Amanda Stevens
When Rae Cavanaugh's niece mysteriously goes missing, county sheriff
Tom Brannon is determined to find her. But as electricity sparks between
Rae and Tom, Rae discovers—despite her misgivings—Tom is the only one
she can trust...

**YOU CAN FIND MORE INFORMATION ON UPCOMING HARLEQUIN TITLES,
FREE EXCERPTS AND MORE AT HARLEQUIN.COM.**

HICNM0520

ReaderService.com has a new look!

We have refreshed our website and
we want to share our new look with you.
Head over to ReaderService.com
and check it out!

On ReaderService.com, you can:

- Try 2 free books from any series
- Access risk-free special offers
- View your account history & manage payments
- Browse the latest Bonus Bucks catalog

Don't miss out!

If you want to stay up-to-date on the latest at the Reader Service and enjoy more Harlequin content, make sure you've signed up for our monthly News & Notes email newsletter. Sign up online at ReaderService.com.